Mistletoe & Marriage

Christmas Kisses, Yuletide Vows

After the deaths of their parents, cousins Penny and Sally must face Christmas alone. But both girls are determined to keep their family alive in their hearts, and pull together. So each prepares for Christmas, but a surprise awaits them both....

Last month…

The Cowboy's Christmas Proposal

Penny Bradford has no idea how to run her family ranch, so she hires rugged rancher Jake Larson to help. Penny knows Jake can be trusted with the ranch…. but what about her heart?

This month…

Snowbound with Mr. Right

When city-slicker Hunter Bedford arrives in Bailey, ruthlessly determined to buy Sally's small-town store, she's furious. The store is all she has left of her family, and she'll never sell. But with the snow falling, Sally finds herself trapped with Hunter—and, what's more, she's beginning to like it….

Christmas is coming, so snuggle up and get ready for two wonderful winter weddings from bestselling author Judy Christenberry that will warm your hearts.

Look out for Judy's next story
Coming Home to the Cattleman
out in May
Only from Harlequin Romance®

JUDY CHRISTENBERRY

Snowbound with Mr. Right

Mistletoe & Marriage

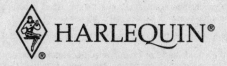

HARLEQUIN®

TORONTO • NEW YORK • LONDON
AMSTERDAM • PARIS • SYDNEY • HAMBURG
STOCKHOLM • ATHENS • TOKYO • MILAN • MADRID
PRAGUE • WARSAW • BUDAPEST • AUCKLAND

ISBN-13: 978-0-373-03991-3
ISBN-10:   0-373-03991-3

SNOWBOUND WITH MR. RIGHT

First North American Publication 2007.

Printed in U.S.A.

Judy Christenberry has been writing romances for fifteen years, because she loves happy endings as much as her readers do. A former French teacher, Judy now devotes herself to writing full-time. She hopes readers have as much fun reading her stories as she does writing them. She spends her spare time reading, watching her favorite sports teams and keeping track of her two daughters. Judy's a native Texan, and lives in Dallas.

CHAPTER ONE

SALLY ROGERS was standing in the window of the Bailey General Store, trying to attain a more attractive display. She was beginning to think it was a lost cause when an idea suddenly struck her. As she began to change the window, she was interrupted by a gentleman she had noticed entering the store earlier.

"Excuse me. I'm looking for the owner of the store."

She looked over her shoulder to see a tall, dignified man, younger than she expected, waiting for her attention.

"Why?" she asked, feeling a little bothered at being interrupted.

"Because I have business to discuss with him."

"Sorry, not right now. The store owner is very busy at the moment," she said. It had been a long day and Sally was tired. She had a lot on her plate with the business, not to mention that she was still coming to terms with the devastating deaths of her parents. Suddenly the store had been left in her hands and she was finding all the decisions to be made to be almost too much.

"I'm sorry, miss, but I don't think that's your decision," the man said sternly.

Sally stepped down from the window, pushing a long strand of blond hair behind an ear. "Actually, yes, it is, and you're interrupting. I just figured out what to do with the window and I really don't have time to stop and talk to you now."

"You?" the man asked in shock. "You're the owner?"

"Yes, I'm the owner." Sally started across the store looking for the item that she knew would work in the window.

To her surprise, the man followed her. "What are you doing?" he asked.

"Not that it's any of your business, but I'm getting the stepladder. It's going in the window."

"The stepladder? Why?" the man questioned.

Sally gave him a wry smile; she obviously wasn't going to get rid of him that easily. "Well, if you must know, I'm going to use it to display some shirts in the window. It needs some vertical lift." She reached for the ladder, but before she could pick it up the man lifted it out of Sally's hands.

"Allow me to carry it for you. And I agree, by the way, this will display the shirts well."

Sally was now getting very annoyed by this man and stood staring at him. "Thank you for offering, but I can carry it myself."

The man smiled at her, obviously not planning on letting Sally win. "Look, I need to talk to you and you are very busy. I'm here, I might as well help out."

Sighing, Sally led the way back across the store to the front window display. She stepped up into the window and then reached for the ladder as he held it up to her. Spreading the legs of the ladder apart she began to hang the shirts on different levels, until she was at last happy with the display.

When she had finished, Sally went outside to see how her efforts looked from the customers' point of view. To her surprise, she found the stranger right beside her as she evaluated the window.

"Nice job. Um, how long have you owned the store?"

"Not long, just since the deaths of my parents."

The man looked at the ground. "No wonder my ownership information wasn't accurate."

Sally said quietly, "Did your ownership information list Bob Rogers as the owner?"

"Yes, that's right. I take it that was your dad?"

"I inherited it when my parents died."

The man stared at Sally. She shrugged. "Sorry, I should've said it more politely, but it's still hard for me to—to go into detail with people. Both my parents were killed in a car crash, along with my aunt and uncle. I've been owner of Bailey's General Store ever since."

"Then what I have to say—I mean, of course you may not want to hold to the agreement. I guess we can talk about it, but I think—"

"Look, I'm tired and I don't know what you're talking about," Sally said with a sigh.

"Your father didn't tell you I'd be coming here?"

Sally turned to stare at the man. He looked like he belonged in a *GQ* ad, not standing in her country store. "My father? How would my father have known that you were coming?"

The man shifted, suddenly looking a little uncomfortable. "He and my grandfather struck up a deal."

"Your grandfather? Who is your grandfather?"

"Wilbur Hunt, of the Hunt Corporation out of Denver." The young man looked as if he expected Sally to be impressed.

"I don't believe I found any letters from the Hunt Corporation for any reason when I went through my father's papers. Certainly not dealing with an arrangement that would—what kind of a deal?"

"I was to work here in the store for your father for the second half of the month."

Sally stared at him as if he'd spoken a second language. "You must be kidding. That's ridiculous!"

"Why is it ridiculous?"

"Because my father has—had enough help for Christmas."

"He wasn't going to pay me a salary. My grandfather had talked to your father about selling the store." He held up his hand when she would've interrupted him. "Your father refused to even consider selling. But because of the amount of business you do, my grandfather thought I might find out good information if we decided to branch out into smaller stores across the state."

"So my father could teach you how to put us out of business? My father wouldn't do that," Sally responded.

"No, they had an agreement that we wouldn't take over any store, or open a new store, within your area."

"I didn't find any such agreement."

"I believe it was a gentleman's agreement."

"I don't think my father would settle for that. It would

have to be in writing. And if not for him, then for me. I wouldn't allow you to work here unless you signed a non-compete clause."

"Sally?" a voice called from the back of the store.

"Coming," she returned. With an apologetic smile, she said, "I have to go see what's wrong. Excuse me."

When she got to the back room, she found her employee, Billy Johnson, standing, looking puzzled.

"What is it, Billy?"

"I don't know what I'm supposed to do with these things, Sally."

She looked at the stack of boxes. They each held jeans. "You put these on the shelves in the men's department, Billy. See? It's jeans."

"But some of them are girls' jeans."

Sally smiled. "Then you put those in the women's department. Here, I'll separate them for you."

Billy had worked in the store for over twenty years. He was a good worker, but at almost seventy he often got a little confused over things. Her dad had said Billy was the hardest worker he'd ever known and he could still be relied on to lift the heavier loads that Sally couldn't manage.

"Oh. Okay. I got it, Sally." Billy nodded as Sally showed him what he needed to do.

She went back into the store to find the stranger still there, leaning against the checkout counter. "Do you need something else?" she asked.

"Just more time to talk to you."

"I'm sorry, but it's Christmas. I really don't have much time to spare."

"Do you have a Christmas rush here, too?" the stranger asked, clearly not ready to leave yet.

"Yes, we do. Our Christmas Festival is in a little over a week from now and we are always busier then. I have a lot to get organized."

"What's the Christmas Festival?" he questioned again.

Sally smiled and decided it might be best to humor him. "Well, it's a town celebration for Christmas. Our parents started it when we were three and it's been going ever since." Sally thought about all the good times she and her cousin, Penny, had shared over the years. This Christmas was going to be hard for both of them.

The man paused before he spoke again. "We? Do you have brothers or sisters?"

"No, I'm an only child. I meant my cousin and I. We both wanted to see Santa when we were very little, but there was nowhere near here where we could go. Our parents decided it would be easier if they brought Santa to our town. They ended up taking turns playing Santa. Now a lot of people come to our Festival for a chance to see Santa."

The man looked at Sally. "And how much money do you make off of it now you're older?"

Sally heard the sarcasm in his voice and turned to face him. He was really beginning to annoy her with all his questions. "Not a penny, actually. In fact we serve refreshments free of charge and offer used clothing and toys to those who need it. Shopping in the store increases naturally, but that's all. My cousin, Penny, will supply the Christmas tree and I'll decorate it. She does some of the baking, along with some other ladies in town who volunteer. It's a true Christmas Festival."

The stranger stood up straight and shifted uncomfortably. "I'm impressed. You could probably make a fair amount of money if you charged for some things, especially the refreshments."

"No, thank you. That's big city talk, not small town talk."

"Maybe. But you could consider—"

"No. We won't change the Festival," Sally insisted, staring the man straight in the face.

"Has anyone ever told you you're stubborn?" the stranger asked with a grin that almost won her over.

Quickly Sally turned away, afraid he would see the tears that his remark had brought. That had been one of her father's frequent complaints about both her and her mother. Except his had been full of love. The sudden memory made Sally's heart ache.

"Hey, what did I say?" the man asked, moving to stand nearer to Sally. "I was only teasing. I didn't mean to make you cry." He put his hand on her arm, tugging her gently to face him.

"It's okay…I'm okay. It's just my father made that complaint frequently," she whispered.

"Damn! I'm sorry. I didn't mean to—most everything around here must remind you of them."

"Yes, it does," Sally answered, quickly wiping away her tears. She didn't want to think about how close she was standing to this strange man, how reassuring his arms felt holding hers and how good he smelled.

The bell over the front door jingled as it opened and a customer came in. Sally moved herself away from the man and composed herself before turning to the customer.

"Good morning, Mrs Ellison. How may I help you?" Sally asked, stepping toward the lady, grateful for the interruption.

"I've come for some of that yarn I bought last week. It's part of a Christmas gift I'm making for my granddaughter."

"Oh, yes, I remember. It's right this way." Sally led the lady to the yarn section and pulled out the exact shade she wanted. "Now, is there anything else I can get you? I just got in some special face cream that you might want to try."

"Really? Will it make my wrinkles go away?"

"It doesn't promise that, but I think it will soften them a little," Sally answered smiling at the elderly lady.

Sally led her to the newest product the store had to offer. Mrs Ellison ended up buying a jar of the cream. And she added two new coloring books, for her granddaughter's Christmas stocking, too.

When she left the store, the stranger was still there.

"Nice job of selling up."

"Thank you," Sally said coolly, wondering why he was still hanging around. "Is there anything I can show you before you leave?"

"Will you have lunch with me?" he asked suddenly, taking Sally by surprise.

Sally stared at the man. "No, I don't leave for lunch."

"Then dinner?"

"This is a busy time of the year."

"You have to eat sometime. I'll find a place to stay and be back about six o'clock. Please? I don't like to eat alone."

Sally knew that she shouldn't get involved with this man. It immediately made her miss her parents, and she felt a sudden stab to her heart. They wouldn't have let her go without a warning. After all, the man was a handsome stranger and new to town. What's more he was a city guy, and had already made it clear that he thought differently to Sally. But she was on her own now and had to make her own decisions. Nervously, she nodded, instinctively trusting that she would be okay with this man, even though she hardly knew him. "There's only one decent restaurant in town. The Diamond Back is one block down. I'll meet you there at six."

"Great. I'll see you then," he said, smiling again and sending shivers down Sally's back. And then he walked out of the store.

All day, no matter how busy she was, Sally couldn't get the man out of her head. Nor could she forget why he was here.

She would never consider training someone to take over the store. With a non-compete agreement, at least she would know that the future of the store would be safe from competition from someone with insider information. She supposed it wouldn't hurt to show someone how she did things and she certainly needed more help, since she was trying to fill the roles of both parents plus her own jobs.

She had two ladies who came in to help her during the day and they at least allowed her to eat lunch if the store wasn't too busy. She had Billy, but he often left at five, since there were no deliveries in the evenings.

Sally lived in a very nice house on the street right behind the store. Her parents had loved its location and it meant she only had to take a very short walk to get to work.

Sally brought her lunch and dinner from home so that she could make sure she was on hand if anything came up.

Today, Sally had been relieved when the time came for her to take her break. She had decided to spend the time working on the store's books, something her father had taught her to do when she was sixteen. Her mind drifted back to the times they had spent making sure the books were all up-to-date and correct. It wasn't that she hadn't expected to own the store—Sally had been fully prepared to take over, but had thought it would happen when her parents retired. Their deaths had come much too soon.

Sally sat staring into space and began to think about her dinner date for this evening. He was certainly a handsome man, but she now realized she didn't even know his name!

It wasn't often that people wandered into Bailey by chance. It was a small town in the northern part of the state. The mountains surrounding Bailey kept it away from the world, and only those who sought out Bailey would come across it.

Which meant the man had been telling the truth about the agreement her dad and Wilbur Hunt had made. Why else would he have come here? Her father had never mentioned anything about his idea to either her or her mother. But then again he hadn't expected to die so suddenly, either.

As the day traveled to its end, Sally began to wonder if she'd made a mistake. Her agreement to have a meal with a man when she didn't know his name was unusual. It was more than unusual. It was unheard of.

As the clock drew near six o'clock, Sally began debating more and more about what to do. Should she stay in the store, not meeting the stranger at the restaurant? He'd know where to find her, but he might be so irritated, he wouldn't come back to the store.

If she went to the restaurant, how would she ask for her dinner partner when she didn't even know his name? The vision of his handsome face floated before her. Sally realized that she did in fact want to go and meet him. It would be a relief to talk to someone not from Bailey. Someone who had seen the world. Or at least more than she had.

Finally she slipped over to her house, the big, lonely house she'd shared with her parents. She removed her denim jeans and sweater and put on a slim black skirt and a knit top that showed some sense of style. She even added a little makeup, though she seldom wore any at the store.

At exactly six o'clock, she walked into the Diamond Back restaurant, looking around, hoping to see the man already sitting at a table. No such luck. She looked at the hostess, Diane Diamond, wife of the owner and someone she knew very well from the store.

"Evening, Diane," Sally said, smiling slightly.

"Your guest is waiting at our best table, Sally. Thanks for bringing us new business," Diane answered, smiling fondly at Sally.

Relieved that she hadn't had to ask any uncomfortable questions Sally released a sigh. "You're welcome, Diane." And moved in the direction the other woman indicated. She rounded the corner and saw a table occupied by the stranger she'd met that morning.

When she approached he stood and moved around the table to hold her chair for her.

"Thank you," she murmured and slid into the seat.

He returned to the seat across from her. As he sat down, he smiled. "You look lovely, Sally."

"How do you know my name?" she asked, taken a little by surprise.

"It's one of the charms of a small town, isn't it? People are willing to talk. Just the hint of your parents' deaths and they told me about you and Penny, your cousin."

"Please don't make fun of small towns. I happen to be fond of them."

"My apologies. I think I neglected to introduce myself this morning. Because of the surprise you handed me, I forgot the niceties. I'm Hunter Bedford and, as I said, I represent the Hunt Corporation of Denver."

"Good evening, Mr Bedford. I'm sorry, but I think you've made a wasted trip," Sally answered, relieved that she at least knew his name now.

Hunter smiled at her again, his perfect teeth gleaming. "I wouldn't say that."

"Mr Bedford, I have only just heard of this arrangement between my father and your grandfather and like I said this morning I'm not interested in training you without a non-compete agreement." Sally was determined that she wasn't going to be railroaded.

"I realize that, not knowing my grandfather, that would be your position. I talked to him on the phone after our meeting this morning and told him of the situation. He was sorry to hear of your father's death and passes on his condolences. He also told me that the agreement they had was a verbal one, between gentlemen, but he has no problem giving you a non-compete agreement if that would make you happier. He is very keen for me to stay here in Bailey and get to know more about your store. And I think you could maybe use some help for the rest of the month—free of charge."

Sally was silent for a moment, thinking about Mr Bedford's words. She knew he was right about the help, but didn't want to appear desperate for him to stay. She said, "We could manage."

They were interrupted by the waitress who stepped up to their table.

"Good evening, folks. Have you had a chance to look at the menu?"

"No, we haven't. Could we have a couple of minutes?"

"Sure thing." The waitress was listening to Sally but was smiling at the stranger.

Sally picked up the menu, though she knew it by memory, to make a decision about what she would eat. Her dinner partner did the same.

After a moment, the waitress reappeared at their table and took their order, both deciding on the meat loaf. "I'll have that right out for you," the waitress said brightly, again smiling at Sally's dinner partner.

"The service here is certainly efficient," he said after the waitress had walked away.

"I believe you think it's because you're a visitor, Mr Bedford, but I suspect it has more to do with your good looks."

"I'll take that as a compliment, Sally, and please, call me Hunter."

"Very well, Hunter. So, what do we have to talk about?"

Hunter smiled. Sally had to admit it was an attractive smile. One that would draw attention anywhere.

"You haven't heard me out. Assuming we have a non-compete clause, would you consider me working in the store?"

Sally took a drink of iced water and returned Hunter's smile. "Tell me, how did you hear of our store? I'm intrigued."

"From our suppliers. The volume of your orders speaks of big sales, larger than a small town store usually handles."

"We have a large range of coverage because there aren't that many towns nearby."

"I noticed that on the map. I even visited some of the stores in the area, what there were of them. But your store is by far the largest and carries the largest range of goods. Why do you suppose that is?"

"I think it has something to do with how long we've been trading for. My grandfather's father opened the store in 1922 and we've grown over the years. Isn't that what stores do when they are successful?"

"Of course it is. And that's why it's attractive to our company. We have five stores in Denver, three in Colorado Springs, and one store each in Pagosa Springs, Fort Collins and Boulder. We want to expand."

"Why don't you consider other states?"

"We've thought of that, but we prefer to keep our properties close together."

"I see."

"Would you be willing to consider hiring me for the rest of the month if we have that non-compete clause in place?"

"I don't know. I'd have to think about it." Sally looked at him intently, his blue eyes seemed genuine and honest and she found herself liking Hunter Bedford more and more.

"You wouldn't be paying me a salary and I promise not to ask too many questions."

"What kind of questions would you ask? I'm new at this myself so I'm not exactly sure what you'd expect to learn."

A wry grin settled across his face. "That's a good point and I don't exactly know myself. I'd have to talk to my grandfather about that."

Their waitress returned with their meal and she immediately asked Hunter if there was anything else he wanted.

"No, thank you, this looks great," he said with another of his special smiles.

The waitress practically floated her way into the kitchen.

"You really should stop flirting with the waitress. She won't be the same...until she realizes it was a one-time visit."

"Will it be?"

Sally stiffened in her chair. "I haven't agreed to anything yet."

"I might hang around anyway, so I can soften you up a little."

Sally took a bite of her meat loaf and chewed it before she answered his suggestion. "I wouldn't think your grandfather would agree to sign a non-compete clause. After all, the area has a lot of appeal, surely he's looking to open nearby?"

"Well, he assures me that he's not interested in competing with you. How long did you say you've owned the store again Sally?"

"It's been in my family since 1922, but running it alone is still all new to me." Sally took another sip of her water and felt the prickle of tears threatening at the back of her eyes.

"You are probably having a hard time handling everything. Why would you turn down some help?" Hunter's voice was gentle.

He'd hit soft tissue. Sally *was* finding herself overwhelmed with all that had happened. Some mornings, she didn't think she'd manage to do everything that had to be done. But why would this man be willing to help her? She was trying to fill three roles—hers, her mother's and her father's. Eventually she'd be able to manage everything. They would hit the slow season after Christmas.

But now?

"Do you think you'd be that big a help?" Sally asked, eager to know more about the man seated in front of her.

"I thought maybe you would be interested in any warm body, at this point, especially at this time of year. And I do have some experience in working in a store."

"You've worked as a salesman in your grandfather's stores?"

"Yeah. He's one of the old school who believe you have to learn from the bottom up."

Sally rolled her eyes. "I take it you didn't enjoy that kind of work?"

"Actually I enjoyed a lot of the jobs. Selling was one of the fun ones. I like people."

"Aren't you anxious to return home to be with your family for Christmas?"

"My grandfather expects me to work until Christmas

Eve. I think I may enjoy working here rather than return-ing to Denver."

"Is your grandfather your only relative?"

Hunter gave a small smile. "My first name comes from the family name. My grandmother is dead. My parents are divorced and have been for a while. My mother probably won't be in Denver for Christmas."

Sally could tell that Hunter found it difficult to talk about his family. "I don't think your grandfather would ap-preciate your staying here until Christmas, Hunter. I bet he'll ask you to come home before Christmas so you can spend the holiday together."

"My grandfather would work everyone until midnight Christmas Eve if it didn't get bad publicity! I'd like to stay on a little longer. What do you think?"

"I'll think about it, Hunter. That's all I can promise you tonight." The evening had been pleasant and Sally had enjoyed Hunter's company more than she thought she would. But could she really let him work at her store every day?

"Okay, you'll see me tomorrow," Hunter said, with a gleam in his blue eyes that Sally just didn't want to think about!

CHAPTER TWO

THE next day, Sally found herself looking forward to going to work. She argued with herself that this was just because she had a lot to do in time for the Christmas Festival and not because Hunter Bedford had promised to return. It shouldn't make such a difference to her life anyway. She'd stalled him, but deep down his promise to come back added a sparkle to going to the store.

Once there, she kept waiting for Hunter to reappear. By noon, she gave up thinking he'd walk in any minute. Obviously she'd convinced him he'd be wasting his time. She had actually considered what he was offering. Having an extra hand in the store would be appreciated, especially if she wasn't paying him a salary.

Of course, the store was doing well enough that she could afford to pay him; she could even give up work herself if she wanted to. Her father had consistently saved a portion of income for the past twenty-five years, investing it in several mutual funds. In addition to the life insurance her parents had carried, the savings were enough to pay for at least twenty years of living well, without working at all. But she knew the store was in her blood.

"Aren't you going to eat your lunch today, Sally?" Mary, one of the ladies who came in to work at the store, asked.

"Oh, yes. I was just daydreaming. I'm going to eat now, Mary, thank you." Sally went to the back room, where a section had been set up for break time, including a table and chairs and a small refrigerator and microwave.

When Sally sat down at the table with her lunch, she told herself she should be glad Hunter Bedford hadn't come back. But she had to admit that his visit had provided a little excitement for her. Something to lift aside the doldrums of her mourning and the pressure she was experiencing. But she could manage on her own. Of course she could.

Just then, Ethel, the other woman who worked for Sally, came into the back room.

"Yes, Ethel? Is there a problem?" Sally asked.

"No, not exactly. But there's a man here who—"

"I'll be right out," Sally said as she jumped up from her chair. So he *had* come back!

She brushed back her hair, hanging loose and flowing today, and hurried out into the store. But there was no terrific smile waiting for her. No snappily dressed man standing around. No sparkle.

Just a farmer dressed in his overalls.

"Hello. Can I help you?"

"Yes, ma'am. I'm Joe Sanders. My wife picked out a gadget she wanted for Christmas and I'm wondering if you could show me what it is?"

"Oh, Mrs Sanders. Yes, of course, I know exactly what she wanted. Come this way with me, please."

"Ma'am, I have a little problem."

Sally stopped and looked at the man. "A problem?"

The man flushed slightly and shifted nervously in front of Sally. "Well, my wife said it costs a hundred dollars and, well, I don't have a hundred dollars. I wondered if you'd consider letting me pay it out. I have thirty-five now, and I can pay thirty-five the next two months. I promise I'm trustworthy."

Sally smiled. "I'm sure you are, Mr Sanders. And yes, I'll sell it to you for thirty-five today and thirty-five in January and February. If that's what you want?"

The man's face turned red. "Yes, ma'am. My wife would be very disappointed if she doesn't get it for Christmas, even though I told her I didn't have the money. I think she still believes in Santa Claus."

"I understand. I'll write out a paper for you to sign. But let me show you what she chose, first."

When the man had seen the gift his wife wanted and signed the paper, paying his thirty-five dollars today and taking his gift with him, Sally returned to her lunch.

The request from Mr Sanders had reminded her again of the importance of the service they provided here at the store. Her father had first introduced a long payment plan about fifteen years ago. Since then, he let it be known that he could trust a few people to pay out their Christmas gifts. After all, her father had said it served the Spirit of Christmas.

It wasn't something that regular stores did. They would let someone pay out the cost of the gift, but they didn't let a customer take home a gift until it was completely paid for.

Sally felt sure Mr Sanders would pay his debt. And she felt good about following in her father's footsteps.

She'd been disappointed that the man waiting for her wasn't Hunter Bedford. She'd thought about him a lot this morning and especially when she had been serving Mr Sanders. She had been sure that a man from the city like Hunter wouldn't have approved of the paying out plan and she would have liked to have talked to him about it. Too bad she wouldn't be able to do that now. That was the only reason she was sad that he hadn't come back, of course.

When the store closed at eight o'clock, Sally went home. She hadn't been in the house more than fifteen minutes when the phone rang. It was probably Penny. She hadn't talked to her since she'd gone out to the ranch for dinner. She moved to the phone. "Hello?"

"Sally?"

"Yes, who's speaking please?"

"It's Hunter. I just wanted to apologize for not coming in today. I had to drive back to Denver today to pick up the non-compete agreement signed by my grandfather. I thought you'd need it in hand before you agreed for me to work in the store. Anyway, I'll be in tomorrow bright and early."

"Hunter, I haven't agreed—"

"Wait until you read what Granddad wrote you and then make your decision."

"Fine. I can certainly find jobs for you if you're willing to work."

"I'm willing. There's just one problem. Your dad was going to provide me with a place to stay. I know that won't work now with just you in the house so I was wondering if there is anywhere in town that I can stay?"

Sally thought for a moment about Hunter moving in here with her. She knew the idea was absurd, but part of her thought about recommending it. But Bailey was a small town and people would certainly talk so instead she said, "There's a bed-and-breakfast in town. It's the only place, but it's very friendly."

"Good. I'll see if they can get me a room, then I'll see you tomorrow. Good night, Sally."

"Good night, Hunter."

Sally hung up the phone, feeling a little breathless at the thought of Hunter returning in the morning. She knew that his visit was only business and to prove this she began to make a list of possible tasks for Hunter to do. She stayed up a little later than normal and got totally involved in thinking up jobs for Hunter. It was an enjoyable thing to think about.

When she finally crawled into bed, she was pleasantly tired and immediately fell asleep. The ringing of the alarm clock the next morning didn't really wake her up. Until the thought of Hunter arriving this morning told her she needed to get out of bed.

Unfortunately this was half an hour after the alarm had gone off and Sally had to dress hurriedly and make her lunch and dinner in less than half the time she usually took. She simply tied back her hair after hastily brushing it and ran the short distance to the store.

Billy was waiting at the back door to get in, and had been for half an hour.

"I'm sorry, Billy. I overslept. You must be cold."

"Naw, I'm wearing a coat," he answered, rubbing his gloved hands together.

"Yes, but take some time to warm up. Make yourself a cup of coffee," Sally replied, feeling bad for keeping the elderly man waiting in the cold.

"Okay, Sally. Would you like one, too?"

"No, thanks, Billy. I'll get one a little later," Sally said as she hurried through the store. Quickly Sally began raising the shade on the front door, ready to start the day. Hunter was standing there.

"I thought you might be here a little earlier than this?"

"I'm sorry, Hunter. I overslept this morning," Sally answered, a little annoyed that his first day had started so badly. What would he think of how she ran things around here?

"Not a problem. I got here a little early, anyway. Are you all right?"

"Yes, I'm fine."

He followed Sally into the store. "So, what needs to be done first?"

"Well, I usually tidy the store from the previous day. You know, straighten all the goods, make sure the dressing rooms are empty and rehang any clothing left in them."

"All right. I'll check the dressing rooms first," he said and made his way over to the other side of the store.

Sally stood looking at him as he walked toward the dressing rooms. Could she have expected him to do the menial tasks as well as the more important ones? She didn't think so, but she began straightening the shelves to make the store look neat and attractive.

Half an hour later, the store was in pristine condition. Sally invited Hunter to join her in a cup of coffee.

"I'd love a cup. I didn't know if you were a coffee drinker," Hunter said with a grin. "But, what if someone comes in to shop?"

"We'll hear the bell over the front door."

"That's something we don't have in a big store," Hunter said.

"I know. But you usually have more customers than I do."

"True."

When they reached the break room, they found Billy still there nursing his cup of coffee.

"Billy, this is Hunter Bedford. He's going to be working here in the store for a couple of weeks. Hunter, this is Billy Johnson. Billy has been with us for a long time and handles most of the heavy work for the store. We couldn't be without him."

"Hi," Billy said, holding out his hand.

"Hello, Billy," Hunter said, returning the man's handshake. "It's good to meet you, too."

"Okay," Billy said. Then he tipped his coffee mug up and finished off the coffee. "I'm going to work now, Sally."

"Thanks, Billy."

Once Billy went back to the delivery area, she said softly, "My dad and Billy were old friends and he always said that Billy was the hardest worker he knew. He's been here for a long time."

"Yeah, I could tell. He seems able to handle almost any delivery all by himself. It's good to have someone like that around, someone you can trust," Hunter said, looking at Sally.

"Yes, it is." For a tiny, short second their gazes locked and Sally found herself melting into his deep blue eyes and a tiny shiver of electricity ran down her spine.

The jingle of the bell interrupted them. Sally automatically stood.

"Let me go," Hunter said.

"No. No one would recognize you just yet. I'll go." She walked out into the store, finally spotting the shopper. Sally had waited on him before.

"Hello, Mr Jackson. How may I help you?"

"Hi, Sally, I need to find a gift for my boss."

He didn't need to tell Sally he worked at the stables on the edge of town. Or that his boss was Mr Gray.

"Well, the last time Mr Gray was in here, he was looking at work gloves. He said his old ones were wearing out. He thought he might buy some after Christmas."

"Perfect. Where are the work gloves?"

"Right this way." She led the way down the aisle and showed him the three different styles.

When he had made his choice, Sally led him to the cash register. "Now, I think I have a box these will fit nicely in," she said and pulled out a red box with a piece of tissue paper. Then she folded the gloves into the box, put the lid on it and put it in a sack.

"There you go, Mr Jackson. And merry Christmas to you."

"Thank you, ma'am. Same to you."

Before he could reach the door, it opened and two ladies came into the store. Sally advanced to the two ladies. "Good morning, ladies. Are you Christmas shopping today?"

"Yes, we are. Our daughters like to get the same thing

at Christmas since they play together. So we're doing some Santa shopping. But we don't need any help. We know this store backward and forward, Sally. We'll bring what we want to the cash register when we're ready."

"Thank you. If I'm not out here, just hit the bell by the cash register."

She headed for the back room, but she didn't reach it before the front door opened again. This shopper was male, and someone she didn't recognize. She stepped to the curtain and called, "Hunter, can you come here please?"

She heard him move to the opening. "A gentleman has just entered the store. I don't know him, so I think it will be a good idea for you to wait on him. It looks like this may be a busy morning."

"Sure. I'll be glad to wait on him, it will give me a chance to get some practice in."

She watched as Hunter walked up to the man and they both moved across the store to the men's department. She realized that it was a good thing to have a male salesperson again. No one had replaced her father, and she wasn't sure anyone ever could, but it was good to have a man on hand. Some of the male customers could be a little shy around women, and others much too flirtatious.

The door opened again, and one of Sally's favorite customers entered the store. "Mrs Grabowski, how are you? Are you staying warm enough?"

"Warm enough? Of course I am. I didn't even make a fire this morning. I just made oatmeal on my little stove," the old lady said. She had been shopping at the store for many years and was a valued customer.

"My, you are certainly spartan. I hugged the stove this morning to get warm."

"Silly girl. Your daddy knows better than to—oh, sorry, Sally, I didn't mean—sometimes I forget things. You're doing fine. I'm here to get some more yarn."

The mention of Sally's father shocked her for a moment, but she quickly pulled herself together. "Right this way, Mrs Grabowski," Sally said, and led the way to the yarn, discussing the various colors available with the elderly lady. Once she had waited on Mrs Grabowski, she dealt with the two lady shoppers who had entered the store earlier and were buying the same gifts for their daughters. She gift-wrapped their items and thanked them for their patronage.

Then Hunter brought the gentleman to the cash register and began putting the garments the man was buying into boxes after Sally had rang up each item. By the time the man paid his bill, a substantial one, his purchases were ready to go.

"Did you find out who he is?" Sally asked.

"You want me to get personal with the man?" Hunter asked, raising his brows.

"I just wondered where he was from, I haven't seen him around here before."

"He just bought the Gibson farm. He and his wife are going to retire here."

"Oh, how wonderful. Tom and Ellen had been hoping it would sell by Christmas. I hadn't heard that they'd managed to sell it. That's great."

"I'm glad I could provide the information to you," Hunter said.

"Well, it is important, Hunter. We're a small community, and we like to keep up with changes in the ownership."

"Shall we print up a newsletter for you to pass out?"

"No. That's not necessary, and I don't appreciate your sarcasm. It's important to know everything about your customers, that way you can help them better." Sally realized she and Hunter came from very different worlds. She was going to have a lot to teach him.

"I was only teasing. Is there a newspaper in town? I'll have to subscribe."

"I think you're making fun of me, Hunter, but yes we do have a newspaper. You can find it in the box right outside the store. You should take a look—you could learn a lot about our customers by studying the paper," Sally answered, slightly annoyed at Hunter's teasing.

"I believe you. And maybe I was making a little fun of you, Sally, but not much. You're too smart, from what I can see, for me to make fun of you."

"Thank you…I think."

He smiled at her. "You can be sure. My parents taught me to recognize a smart person."

Before Sally could say anything in reply, Mary and Ethel arrived for work. She introduced Hunter to them, explaining that he was going to be working for her for the next couple of weeks.

Hunter immediately turned on his smile and expressed pleasure in meeting them and both ladies melted at once.

Sally suggested they show Hunter around as he was just learning the departments and they both beamed agreeing this would be a good idea. Sally walked away from the threesome, pleased to have time alone. At least, that's what she told herself.

Settling down with the store's accounts, she caught up on the entries and made the calculations as necessary. Then she closed the books and put them away. Once that was done, she got out her lunch and began to eat alone. She didn't go out on to the floor to figure out what was taking so long with the tour of the store. She figured she could check on the threesome after she ate her lunch.

When she did finally go out on the floor, she discovered the store was full of shoppers. Sally realized that she must have been daydreaming as she hadn't heard the bell ring once. As she looked around she could see that all three of her salespeople, including Hunter, were helping someone, and there were others waiting. Sally immediately assisted those waiting and having made an inroad on these customers, she looked up to see where the other three were working. She could see that they had each taken other shoppers so Sally went to the cash register and began ringing up sales.

Every time she rang up sales by another person, she marked the ticket by using the initials of the salesperson. If she didn't remember, she would ask the purchaser who helped him or her. A lot of purchasers were willing to name their salesperson. Those who couldn't would only say they had a man wait on them so they had to have had Hunter.

Several hours later, they finally had a lull and Sally sent both ladies to have a cup of coffee. "Even if we get busy again, I think Hunter can take a break if the three of us are on the floor."

"Of course," Mary said. "But will Hunter be able to make his cup of coffee?"

"He'd better be, or he won't get any to drink."

Hunter gave her a lazy grin. "Don't fret about it, Sally. I can make a cup of coffee."

"I felt sure you could."

She turned her back on him, hoping she could hide the wave of attraction that ran over her when he smiled.

"Going somewhere?" he asked.

"No, I was just looking over the store. I think the jeans section needs straightening."

"I'll be glad to take care of it."

"No! I—very well. Thank you."

Hunter strolled to the jeans section and began straightening it.

Sally looked around the store and found another section that required attention. She needed something to stay busy, otherwise, she'd be staring at Hunter all day! He had a particularly graceful style about him as he worked.

Sally remembered a young man who had once been in Bailey temporarily because he'd been banished to his grandparents by his parents. Sally had thought herself in love with him at one time, but her father had warned her that pretty is as pretty does. Did Hunter know that expression? Or was he used to proving his way, rather than charming his way?

She'd vote for charming. It was in his genes, she thought, and not the jeans he was sorting. It was obvious he could turn on his charm at a moment's notice.

Sally decided that maybe it was time to put Hunter

Bedford in his place. He'd said that he would stay until Christmas Eve, but maybe it would be better if he only stayed for a few days. Then he could return to Denver, the big city, never to return to Bailey.

The phone rang and Sally hurried to answer. It wasn't often that they had phone calls. "Bailey General Store," she said cheerfully.

"Is this Sally Rogers?"

"Yes, it is. How may I help you?"

"Hello, Miss Rogers, this is Wilbur Hunt. I hope my grandson is behaving himself."

Sally smiled at the voice on the other end of the line. "Hello, Mr Hunt. Yes, he is. He's being very helpful, actually."

"Good. I'm glad to hear it. Could I speak to him, please?"

"Just a moment, please." She put down the phone and turned to call Hunter to the phone.

"Me?" he asked in surprise.

"It's your grandfather."

Hunter frowned and made his way to the phone, taking the receiver from Sally.

"Hello, Granddad?"

Sally moved to a department as far away as possible. Even though she strained her ears, she couldn't hear what he said to his grandfather. Maybe the man was recalling him. That would certainly solve her problem, but the thought suddenly made her feel a little sad.

Hunter hung up the phone. "Sorry about that."

"Not a problem. When do you have to leave?"

"I'm not going anywhere. Why would I?"

"Oh, I assumed that's why your grandfather called."

Hunter gave her his lazy grin again. "Not hardly. He actually wanted to know if you were working me. He thinks it's important that I earn my keep."

"I wanted to talk to you about that. We've been very busy today, so I intend to pay you the same as I'm paying Mary and Ethel—it's only fair."

"I wasn't talking about a wage, Sally. I don't expect you to pay me. I'm here to learn about your business for my own benefit."

"Well, you will definitely work hard during the two weeks you'll be here if today is anything to go by. We have been very busy already."

"Well, I'll be happy to do anything you ask me to. Just say the word."

Sally suddenly thought of something he could do that neither lady could do for her and which had been troubling her for some time now. "Actually, Hunter, I do have an additional way you can help me."

"Sure. Like I said, I'll be glad to do anything. What do you have in mind?"

Sally smiled, knowing that this request would at least take Hunter by surprise. "I'll need you to play Santa."

CHAPTER THREE

HUNTER stared at her. "What did you say?"

"I'll need you to play Santa. Remember, I told you that my dad and my uncle used to play Santa every year. Well, this year we don't have anyone."

Hunter paused a moment while he digested this information. Then he said, "But I'm not good with kids," his expression earnest.

"I'm sure you'll learn fast enough," Sally replied, sensing Hunter's resistance.

"Sally, I think you should find someone else, someone more used to little kids. And besides, I don't have a Santa suit."

"But I do. You're about the same size as Dad, except for his weight. He'd put on a few pounds but we can disguise that with pillows. It will look great on you."

"And you expect me to go out there all by myself and play Santa? Don't I even get a helper?"

"I'm sure you'll do fine on your own, Hunter."

"Oh, no, I'll need a Santa's helper. Like you, for example. Then I could play Santa." Hunter smiled, if playing Santa meant spending more time with Sally, then maybe it wasn't such a bad idea.

Sally tensed a little, sensing that her good idea was maybe turning into a bad move. "Hmm, we'll see. I'll have to think about it."

"Come on, Sally. What's to think about? Unless you're scared to go out there with me."

"Of course I'm not scared! But I just don't see how a helper is necessary. You listen to what the children want and say you'll do what you can. No promises. That's against the rules. Then they take a picture and leave."

"Pictures? They'll take pictures? But it will ruin my image!"

"Exactly what image are you trying to portray?" Sally asked, feeling that Hunter was teasing her again.

Just as he was going to tell her, the door jingled, and several shoppers came in. "Later," Hunter promised and went to offer assistance to the shoppers.

Sally watched him smile at the customers and knew he was going to do fine as a salesperson. He seemed willing to guide them through the store. Mary and Ethel must've done a good job showing him around.

Suddenly she realized Hunter was signaling her and Sally hurried over to greet the shoppers.

"Can I help?" she asked Hunter.

"Mr Carson's wife here would like to have some assistance in the men's department."

"Certainly, Mrs Carson. How can I help you?"

"I need to buy someone's present," the woman said, motioning in her husband's direction.

"Ah, let's discuss it over here," Sally said, leading the woman away from her husband and Hunter. "Do you have anything in mind?"

The lady had plenty of ideas and Sally showed her all the possibilities. When they'd looked at everything, Mrs Carson decided on a small, portable television.

Sally suggested some other shopping the woman might need to do, in case her husband hadn't finished with his shopping.

"I really don't feel like shopping anymore. I did my Christmas shopping early for everyone except Mr Difficult."

"Then why don't you join me for coffee? That will give them the entire store to shop." Sally led the way to the break room and fixed two cups of coffee. Then she sat down at the table with her customer and they discussed the goings-on in the town. Sally reminded Mrs Carson about the Christmas Festival and asked if she had any contributions to donate.

"You know, come to think of it, I believe I do. I'm glad you mentioned it, Sally. I've got some toys that don't have any wear and tear. And some clothes, too. I'll be glad to bring some things to be given away."

"Oh, good. I'll—yes, Hunter?" Sally stopped talking as she noticed Hunter standing by the doorway.

"Sorry to interrupt your coffee, ladies, but Mr Carson wondered if his wife is finished shopping?"

"Yes, I am," Mrs Carson said, smiling at Hunter.

Since Sally had covered the gift Mrs Carson had purchased, all Mr Carson had to do was carry the package for his wife. The couple left the store, both smiling.

"That worked well," Hunter said as he took Mrs Carson's place at the table.

"Yes, they're a very nice couple, old friends of Mom and Dad. I was reminding Mrs Carson about the Christmas Festival. She's going to donate some things."

"Who takes care of donations like that?"

"We do."

"We who?"

"We do. People bring things to the store and we have to sort through them and decide if the donations are up to par."

Hunter shook his head. "How will you have time to do all that work when we're so busy with customers?"

"Not take as many coffee breaks?" Sally asked with a smile.

"I kind of like coffee breaks, especially taking them with you."

Sally was silent for a moment and she sensed something in the air between her and Hunter. "Maybe I'll just assign the task to you," she said.

"I think I'll do better with the customers."

"You're probably right."

"You make that sound like a bad thing."

"No, I—" She was interrupted by the jingle of the door again. "I'll go," he said and got up and walked out into the store. Mary and Ethel could probably handle it, but Sally was glad to have a break from Hunter. Something happened to her whenever he was close and if she wasn't careful, she'd give him anything he asked for.

Getting up, she went to the back loading dock. "Billy? Are you busy?"

"No, Sally. I'm just waiting for another delivery."

"I see. Do you think you could go to our storage area and bring down the decorations for the town tree and bring them into the break room."

"Okay, Sally. Whatever you say."

Sally sighed. It was so much easier to deal with Billy. He was happy to do whatever she wanted. She relied on him so much, even though he didn't help out with any customers, he gave her the opportunity to manage the store, without having to worry about what was going on behind the scenes. She could think through any difficulties and figure out what to do, but she couldn't always do them on her own.

Hunter was a different proposition. Sally almost lost control when she faced Hunter. Not physical control, though she could see that happening. But she couldn't think straight when she was around the man without really working at it.

She began pacing the break room, trying to think about what else she had to do today. Her cousin, Penny, had promised to donate the Christmas tree for the Festival. Sally would have to get Billy to put a stand on the tree and get it secured in the town center. Then she'd need help decorating it, which would probably take up a lot of her time. She'd have to make sure that the store had enough cover whilst she was busy doing that.

Billy brought in several boxes of ornaments and Sally knew there would be several more, at least. The ornaments were large-size so they would show up on the tree.

"Thanks, Billy, You're a real help!"

"Okay, Sally."

Fortunately, okay was Billy's favorite word. He used it anytime she asked anything of him and she smiled. Too bad Hunter didn't adapt Billy's agreeableness.

"What's causing that smile?" Hunter suddenly asked, stepping into the break room.

"Just a pleasant thought," Sally said. "Is there a problem out there?"

"No, not really. The ladies said I should ask you, but I think I already know the answer."

"What's the question?"

"Do I work on the weekends?"

"Did you have other plans for this weekend?"

"No."

"Then yes, it would be great if you could work on Saturday."

"Okay." He stared at her when a big smile appeared on her lips. "Why such a big smile?"

"I was, uh, thinking of something else."

"Is Saturday your busiest day?"

"Yes, it is. Also, we should get the town tree early next week and I'll probably need Billy's help with that. If we get deliveries, you might need to handle those."

"Okay. So I'll need to wear rough clothes then?"

Sally fought the smile that wanted to meet his remark. He had dressed in nice slacks and a dress shirt in the store. She guessed rough clothes meant jeans, which almost everyone who came into the store wore.

"You might want to wear jeans."

"All right. I can do that."

"Thank you, Hunter."

He turned to go back to the main part of the store. She watched him go, wondering what he'd look like in jeans. He had a body that he'd obviously developed through workouts. She felt sure he'd look very good in jeans.

There she went again, her mind on Hunter, rather than her work. She had a lot to do today so they'd be ready for the Christmas Festival. But she really wasn't in the mood for Christmas.

It would be her first one without her parents.

Billy entered the room with more boxes.

"Put them over here, Billy. We'll make stacks of them so I can go through them and check on all the ornaments."

After Billy left the room, Sally took the lid off the top box. Each year, her mother would pack the ornaments to be used the next year. And each year, she, with her mother, had added several ornaments. They made most of them themselves. The large ornaments weren't easy to find.

The top ornaments, wrapped in bubble wrap, were the new ones they'd made the year before. Those ornaments were in good shape. She smoothed her fingers over her favorite one. She'd made it in November last year, with no knowledge of the events that would follow and ultimately end her parents' lives.

Tears filled her eyes. She'd been so happy last year. It had been a good Christmas for all three of them. Her parents had always made her feel so loved. They'd wanted more than one child, but her mother had had several miscarriages and the doctor had warned them that another pregnancy would be difficult. So Sally had been their only child, well loved, but taught the responsibility of being the future owner of the store. She hoped her parents had taught her everything she'd need to know. She wanted to make them proud of her.

"What's that?" Hunter asked as he returned to the break room and broke her daydreaming.

"These are ornaments for the town tree."

He moved to her side to be able to see what she was holding. "That's beautiful. Where do you buy them?"

"Mostly we make them. I made this one last year, but I may not get any made this year."

"Why not?" Hunter asked softly.

"It—it's too time-consuming. I have a lot on my plate this year what with—with all that's happened. I think we'll have enough anyway. We've made quite a lot the last few years and replaced the old ornaments along the way."

"How can I help?"

Sally sniffed and fought off the tears that had earlier threatened. She didn't want Hunter to see her upset. "Once we have the tree up do you think you could help me decorate it? We could start on Thursday and Friday of next week and have it done in time for the Festival on Saturday night."

"Okay. Do you put lights on the tree?"

"Yes. That's the trickiest part of decorating the tree. We leave them on until January 2. It's a little more expensive, but Dad thought it would be nice to have the lights on until then."

"Who pays the bill?"

"We get a discounted rate, but we pay the bill."

"Does that come out of the profit of the store? Can't you write it off as a business expense?"

"Of course. It is a business expense, but we feel it is important." Sally was again reminded of the difference between Hunter and herself. He seemed to be always thinking about how things affected the business, instead of doing it just for the sake of doing it. Maybe that was the difference between big city living and small town life. Sally knew which she preferred.

"I need to decorate the store, too," Sally continued. "We have to have a store tree, as well as garlands and wreaths. I'll ask Billy to bring that out, too. It will take up a lot of space in here, but it shouldn't be for too long. I hope you and the ladies won't mind a little crowding."

"Of course not. I'd wondered about the store—I thought maybe you'd forgotten about it. Granddad always puts up elaborate decorations, too. I guess it's expected."

"No, I hadn't forgotten. I'd just put it off. Everyone's been very understanding, but life goes on. I have to decorate, just like Mom and Dad did. I'm glad you're willing to help."

"If we're too busy tomorrow because of customers, we can decorate it on Sunday. I won't have anything else to do and I'll be honored to help you out."

"Thanks, Hunter. That's very generous." Sally smiled and felt a warm feeling in her stomach. Maybe this Christmas wasn't going to be too bad after all.

He turned to go back to work. "It's beginning to get pretty busy. Do you want to take a moment alone? If you'd prefer, I'll tell the ladies you're busy back here and you can't come."

"No, I'm fine and I'll be right out."

It didn't take long helping customers to find out that a

snowstorm was expected sometime in the early morning of Saturday. That explained the rush. A snowstorm would mean almost no customers tomorrow. In fact, she might not open the store until the storm ended. She'd have to warn the others not to come until they could travel to the store in comfort.

When closing time came, there were still a number of customers shopping. Sally asked them politely if they could decide on their purchases so she could close the store.

"Your daddy never rushed us," a lady complained.

"I'm sorry, ma'am, I guess I'm not as patient, but there's only one of me. Before we had three people who could stay as long as you needed us to."

"No, I'm sorry, Sally," the lady said, flushing slightly. "It's hard sometimes to think that your daddy is gone and that they are really dead. I guess you don't usually forget that, do you?"

"No, I don't. But I'll try to be more patient, like Dad was. He loved running the store."

"Yes, he did and we know you're doing the best you can."

"Thank you, Mrs Crawford. You're being very generous."

The lady paid for her purchase and smiled at Sally. "You know, each day will get easier. That old sun keeps coming up, no matter what."

"Yes, it does. Good night," Sally said, and watched as the last customer left the store.

"Was she giving you a hard time?" Hunter asked softly, pausing beside Sally.

"No, she was just remembering how it used to be when my mom and dad were here. I hadn't realized how much their deaths had affected other people in the town."

They were both silent for a moment and then Hunter spoke. "Well, one thing we can do to make things easier for everyone is to get this store decorated. We can put most of them up tomorrow if there's going to be a snowstorm. We won't have that many customers."

"That's true, but don't try to come to work until the storm has blown through."

"Hmm. I'll see."

"Hunter, what do you mean?"

"I'll probably come over at the regular time, which is nine o'clock, right?"

"But I might not be here. At least call before you come."

"Okay, I'll do that. Now, how about dinner?"

"Do you intend to bring your dinner tomorrow?" Sally asked, not sure what he was asking.

"No. I mean will you have dinner with me, tonight?"

"Oh, no, I don't think so, Hunter."

"Oh come on, you know I don't like to eat alone. Won't you take pity on me?" He looked at her with a pleading look and Sally smiled despite herself.

"I don't think you'll be alone very long. I think you're already meeting a lot of people. I'm sure someone will join you."

"You're telling me that you prefer to eat alone? I don't believe you."

Sally stared at him in frustration. "No, I don't like to eat alone, but it's not good to eat out all the time."

"Then let me cook for you. I'll use your kitchen and make supper for both of us."

"You can cook?" she asked.

"Yeah, I'm pretty good, too. I'll pick up some things and then I'll meet you back at your house. Deal?"

"I—I suppose so."

"Good." To her surprise, he leaned forward and kissed her cheek. "I'm looking forward to it."

She didn't move for several minutes. She'd been used to loving parents who hugged and kissed her frequently. But, with their deaths, no one touched her, unless she visited Penny. And certainly not another man! She thought she should tell Hunter that he shouldn't kiss her, but she knew she liked it.

Too much. But she knew she would have to say something to Hunter. He couldn't go around kissing her like that and she didn't want him trying to get close to her because of the store.

But he was leaving in two weeks. Sally thought how her mother would have teased her about falling for someone who wouldn't stay around, and her father would give her a stern lecture.

But they weren't here and she was on her own. Should she let Hunter get close to her, share time with her? No, of course not. Not when there was a chance, a big chance, he would disappear, returning to the big city, and she'd never see him again. Sally had suffered enough loss recently, and she didn't want to go through that ever again. She knew that she and Hunter would have to keep things strictly business.

Fortunately her sad thoughts were interrupted by Mary and Ethel, coming to retrieve their coats and say goodbye. She told them to feel free to stay home until the storm ended.

They agreed and departed.

Sally looked at the empty store, things in disarray, shelves needing to be straightened, dressing rooms needing to be cleaned. She made a quick check of the dressing rooms, returning merchandise to the open floor and then she turned off the lights, locked the front door and slipped out the back entrance, locking that too. Slowly she walked across the street to the big house. It was such a nice house, made for a large family. Maybe someday she'd have children. She hoped so. She could take the baby to the store with her and take care of it and the store at the same time.

She unlocked her front door and entered the house, looking at it with Hunter's eyes. He was used to Denver. Did he live in a condo, or have a house? Maybe he lived in a big family home with expensive furniture and servants. But she loved her home, with its comfortable furnishings.

A cold draft reminded her about the storm. She put some logs in the fireplace and added kindling. It only took a couple of minutes to get a fire started. After all, she'd been taught by the best fire builder in the county, her father. He'd loved a fire and it added warmth to an already cozy room.

She took off her coat and hung it up. Then she continued into the kitchen. She'd left it clean this morning. Her mother's influence. She never liked to leave a mess in the kitchen. Both parents had taught her so many things.

The doorbell rang.

Drawing a deep breath, she turned to welcome Hunter into her world.

She swung open the door, only to find Billy standing there.

CHAPTER FOUR

"OH, BILLY, is something wrong?"

"There's a storm coming, Sally," the elderly man reminded her.

"Yes, I know. But like I told the others don't try to come in until you can. We'll manage fine."

"Okay, Sally. Do you have everything you need here? You'll be warm enough?"

"Yes, of course. You don't need to worry about me, Billy," Sally said, touched at the old man's thoughtfulness.

"I know, but your daddy said I was to watch over you."

Sally's breath caught. "When—when did he say that?"

"Oh, a few times, but we talked just before he died. It kind of got to me, especially now he's gone."

Billy's eyes misted with tears and Sally reached out and placed a hand on his arm. "Billy, I'll be fine, I promise, but I appreciate your thinking of me."

"I'll keep an eye on her for you, Billy," Hunter said, suddenly appearing behind the older man. "I'll make sure she's warm."

"Hunter," Billy said, spinning around to face the younger

man who had just approached. "I didn't realize you would be here. As long as I know she's all right that's all that matters. I'll leave you two alone now. Have a good night."

"Good night, Billy, and thanks for checking on Sally." Hunter's face was solemn and he nodded to Billy.

"Good night, Billy," Sally called as he left.

Hunter stood there on the porch, watching Billy leave.

"Does he often come check on you?" he asked as he stepped into her home.

"No. I think hearing about the storm worried him, especially with me being on my own now."

"That was thoughtful of him," Hunter said. He began to remove his leather coat as he took in his surroundings. "This is nice, Sally."

"Thank you. Mom did all the decorating."

"You must've shared a lot with your mother, because this reminds me of you."

"Thank you. That's a nice compliment."

"Not one that most women want to hear." He retrieved the sack he'd set on the floor to remove his coat. "Lead the way to the kitchen."

"Follow me." She reached the kitchen and turned on the light. "I think everything you need will be in here. Mom liked every kitchen gadget she'd ever seen. She was constantly ordering things for the kitchen."

"Terrific. I got us a couple of steaks, some broccoli and potatoes to bake."

"It sounds like my favorite meal." She got out a grilling pan for the steaks. "The condiments are over here."

Then she took the potatoes and washed them and rubbed

them with butter before wrapping them in tinfoil. "Would you like a steamer for the broccoli?"

"You're a great assistant, young lady. Usually, when I cook, the lady strolls into the living room and watches television. All that's left to do is to get the steaks cooking. Then we can both go into the living room."

"Let me put on some coffee. It will be enjoyable sitting in the living room by the fire after we've eaten."

"That sounds terrific. This is certainly a lot nicer than the room I'm staying in."

"Mrs Brady has a nice bed-and-breakfast," Sally said.

"Yeah, but it's not like having your own place. I have my own place in Denver, but it's not as scenic as it is here in Bailey. The views from my condo are strictly city, except for the Rockies on the west side."

"You don't live with your grandfather?"

"No, I don't. I used to live with my parents, but they got a divorce. My mother and I moved in with my grandparents. I moved out once I finished college."

She plugged in the coffeepot. "A lot of young people move out of their parents' home after college."

"You didn't want to?" he asked.

"No. I was thrilled to come back home after college. I asked my parents if they wanted me to move out, but they both refused to even consider such a thing."

"That's nice. What did you major in—marketing?"

"Yes. But Dad was ahead of a lot of the things they were teaching us. I learned more working at the store than I ever did at college."

"Yeah. I majored in marketing also. My dad didn't want

me to have anything to do with Granddad's stores. But Mom had been telling me they would be mine one day. There wasn't anything else I wanted to do."

"So what are you doing here, Hunter?"

"I wanted to experience different aspects of running a store. And my grandfather had already spoken to your father about me possibly coming here, and the rest is history."

"Which explains why you came to my store. It doesn't explain why you're staying for two weeks."

"Granddad wanted me to see how you operated. Your store is the best run of any I've seen. If you operate it differently than the other stores, maybe I can use some of your techniques. I've already noticed you carry better stock, in greater volumes."

"When you carry a bigger volume, you can improve the quality of the item because of your volume."

"But why do you have so much business?"

"We're the only store in the area. This is a ranching and farming community. They don't do a lot of frivolous shopping. When they need something, however, they need it immediately from the closest store. And that's us."

"The steaks are ready to go in the oven. On broil, I think."

Sally took the grill pan from him and slid it into the lower oven. Then she turned on the oven as he'd asked. She moved to the counter. "Here's a steamer for the broccoli."

Once the broccoli was on, Hunter looked at Sally. "How about we go sit by the fire until the food needs our attention?"

Though Sally suddenly discovered she was nervous, she agreed. What were they going to talk about?

But Hunter made it easy. He asked about her childhood, talking about his life, also. Then he moved to her college life. "Did you date in college?"

"Yes, of course."

"And you didn't find anyone you wanted to marry?"

"No. Did you?"

"No. I found some who wanted my grandfather's money by marrying me, but I wasn't interested."

"Surely they didn't tell you that!"

"No. They were a bit more subtle."

She smiled at him. "They must've been upset when you told them no."

"Yeah. But a marriage has to be between two people who care about each other. Not one who cares and one who cares about the money they can get."

"Yes, I guess so. I just didn't find anyone who understood what I wanted, or who wanted to live in Bailey. They wanted bright lights, a big city life. That's not for me."

He smiled. "Not tempted?"

She shook her head. "I have what I want, right here. Mom and Dad provided me with an income and a house."

"That sounds a little lonely."

"I suppose so. But I'm surrounded by people I know. And Penny is only a short distance away."

"I haven't met her yet."

"No. She—she's busy with the ranch right now."

"Do you see her often?"

"I had dinner with her last week."

"Is she a good cook?"

"Yes, she is," Sally said with a smile. "But she's hired

a housekeeper because she's trying to learn ranching and stays in the saddle most days."

Hunter winced. "That sounds painful."

"Not for Penny. She's been riding since she was little."

"Do you ride?"

"Yes, I've ridden some. When I go out to the ranch, I ride. Or I used to. Now, I'll be here most days." She unconsciously sighed.

"You could sell." He said the words so softly that Sally was unsure whether she had heard him right. She suddenly had a horrible feeling that Hunter was here under false pretences, and the thought made her sick to her stomach. Sally jumped to her feet.

"Is that why you wanted to cook for me tonight, Hunter? To soften me up? I'm not interested in selling the store, Hunter, and if that's the only reason you are here then you might as well leave now!"

"I didn't mean—you just sounded so stressed. I'd better go check the steaks." Hunter got up and walked back into the kitchen.

Sally sank down onto the sofa. She hadn't meant to chase him away. But she couldn't help it. She had no intention of selling her store ever, but Hunter had been right about one thing. She had been feeling a little burdened by everything that had happened.

"Sally?" Hunter called from the kitchen.

She didn't want to go to the kitchen. Sitting by the fire had seemed so nice. With another sigh, she stood and walked into the kitchen. "Yes?"

Hunter was leaning against the kitchen counter and

looked very handsome in the soft light. He stood and walked nearer to Sally, reaching out to place his hand on her arm. "You're still angry with me?"

Sally immediately felt the familiar prickle of electricity where his hand touched her. "Yes, Hunter, I am." But she didn't move his hand from her arm.

"Sally, I didn't intend to suggest—you just sounded so tired, it seemed like a good idea."

"I am tired a lot right now, but I'd never sell."

"Okay, I've got it. I'm sorry if I upset you. That was the last thing I ever wanted to do. Friends?"

Sally knew that she shouldn't be angry with Hunter. He was just expressing his opinion and she had probably overreacted. They had been getting on well before then and she had been enjoying the time she had spent with him. She walked to the upper oven where the potatoes were cooking. "Okay, friends. These will probably need another fifteen minutes," she said, motioning toward the potatoes and swiftly changing the subject.

Hunter smiled, glad that Sally had forgiven him. "Okay, the steaks should be ready then, too."

Sally turned and took out place mats and put them on the table. Then she got silverware and set the table, adding two plates. Next she made some iced tea and poured it into two glasses with ice. Adding napkins, she stood back and checked the table.

"We'll need butter for the potatoes," Hunter pointed out.

She added the butter, but she also added some shredded cheese and sour cream.

"Do you think the broccoli is done?"

"You're the cook," she said a little stiffly.

"Yeah, but—okay, I'll take the broccoli up." Hunter sensed that maybe he still needed to make amends.

Sally watched as he did that task. Then he turned to the steaks again. When he closed the lower oven to let the steaks cook a little longer, there was nothing left to do for the moment.

"Want to go back to the fire?" he asked.

"No, thank you." She sat down at the table.

He pulled out the chair at the other place setting and sat down across the table from her. "Are we going to talk to each other like before?"

Sally stared at him. "Sure, we can talk. As long as it doesn't involve me selling up."

"What happens when you marry?" Hunter asked.

"What do you mean?"

"What if you fall for someone who lives, say, in Denver?"

"I don't think I could marry anyone who doesn't agree to move here and help me run the store."

"That's seems a little limiting, doesn't it?"

Sally stood, suddenly wanting Hunter to leave. His questions were getting a little too personal and she didn't want to think about the answers. "I can fix your dinner in a disposable plate and wrap it in foil. It will be ready in five minutes."

"Sally, I was just asking a question. Have you thought about these things?"

"Of course I have! But it's really none of your business, Hunter!"

"I was asking as a friend, that's all."

"I don't think we can be friends, not with our working arrangement. I think it was a mistake to let you come here tonight."

"Come on, Sally, the food is almost ready now. Can we just enjoy our meal and put business on one side?"

"No talk about the store?"

"None, I promise," he said and made a cross over his heart.

Sally smiled at his determination and wondered at his ability to win her round so easily. "Fine," she said and swatted him away with her hand.

Hunter got up and took out the steaks, adding the baked potatoes and bringing the broccoli to the table. "Oops, I forgot to put in the bread. It won't take much time."

Sally sat silently as he slid the bread in the oven.

"It will take five minutes. Do you want to start eating?"

"No. It's fine, I'll wait." The food smelled wonderful and Sally realized that she was actually very hungry.

Hunter sat back down and looked at Sally across the table. "Have you traveled much?"

"No, not really. I've always been here."

"Granddad sent me to Europe after I graduated from college. It was quite an experience."

"Where did you go?" Sally asked, grateful for something to talk about besides the store.

"I started in London. It took me a while to understand those people, though they claimed they were speaking English," he said with a laugh. "But I enjoyed it there and spent a bit more time in England taking in a few other sights."

"Did you see Stonehenge?"

"Yeah. A bunch of tall rocks in a circle. But there's

something there—I mean, you get a weird feeling when you're standing in the center of those rocks."

Sally shivered. "Really? I've wondered about that."

"Yeah, I didn't believe it would do anything to me, but it did."

"What about Shakespeare's house?"

"I saw that. It wasn't very big," he said with a grin. "But things were different then, weren't they?"

"Yes, I guess they were."

The buzzer went off. Hunter jumped up and took the golden-brown rolls out of the oven and put them on a plate. He brought them to the table and sat down. "Now we can eat."

Sally nodded her head and then bowed it. She said a short prayer, one her father always said before eating.

When she raised her head, she discovered Hunter watching her. "Is something wrong?"

"Not at all. Broccoli?"

"Yes, thank you."

She served herself and then cut open her potato and added butter, cheese and sour cream. After adding one of the hot rolls and buttering it, she was ready to eat.

A few bites later, she said, "I want to thank you for cooking for me tonight. I'll admit that I don't always eat the way I should because it seems silly to cook for just one."

"My grandfather is a hard worker, but he always says that it's due to the good food my grandmother served every night."

"And your mother?"

"Mom was a society lady. She went to parties and the opera, the symphony, the theater. Five nights out of seven, she was gone."

"But she had to feed you dinner, didn't she?"

"No. The housekeeper fed me. I ate well, but I ate by myself."

"That's sad, Hunter."

"When Mom and Dad got a divorce and we moved in with my grandparents, Mom still went out all the time, but I ate with my grandparents. We had nice dinner conversation and my grandmother taught me good manners."

Sally grinned at him. "She certainly did a good job."

"Yeah. Now I'm grateful. At first I hated it. But having dinner with other people, people who cared about you and took the time to show you how to behave was a great experience."

"That's wonderful."

"I took the time to tell her how much I appreciated all she'd taught me one weekend when I came home from college. I'm glad I did. She died shortly afterward."

"Oh, I'm sorry," Sally said and stopped to look at Hunter more thoughtfully.

Almost as if he didn't hear her words, he said, "I still have my granddad. And my mother and father are still living."

"Yes," she agreed and took a bite of her steak. There were several things she could say, but she wasn't going to.

After a moment of silence, he said, "I'm sorry, Sally, I didn't think."

"It's all right, Hunter."

"No, it was insensitive. Let's talk about something else. If you could go anywhere, where would you want to go?"

"Paris. I took French in college and I've always wanted to see Paris."

"It's a beautiful city. I enjoyed it a lot. But not speaking French is a hindrance."

"Didn't you take it in college?"

"No, I took German. My dad's choice, I might add."

"So did you travel in Germany?"

"Yeah, and it's a beautiful country, but I enjoyed Paris a lot more."

"Did you go to the top of the Eiffel Tower?"

"Yeah. It looks like fun, but it's a long way up. I'm not a great fan of heights and I was worried that I might fall from the top!"

"That's a terrible thought! I think we need to change the subject again. What did you like best about France?"

"The pain au chocolat. I had one of those my first morning in Paris. Every day after that, I had a pain au chocolat. I miss those."

"Yes, I've heard of those, and the croissants. I've been to La Madeleine in Denver. That's the closest I've gotten."

"I didn't know you'd been to Denver."

"Yes, my mom and I would occasionally go shopping in Denver. Mom didn't like to leave Dad all alone, but twice a year we'd make the trip."

"Did you ever spend the night there?"

"A couple of times, but Mom didn't like to stay over."

"I wish I'd known you then. I could've shown you around."

"I saw the stores. In fact, I shopped in one of yours. The one located near the center of downtown."

"Ah. That was Granddad's first store. It grew over the years. Then he began spreading out. But that store is still his favorite."

"It's a marvelous store and the choices are incredible. But most of them wouldn't sell here."

"True. Can't you see a rancher's wife dressed in a zebra-striped dress and spike heels?"

"Actually there are one or two who wear that kind of dress, but they don't fit in well here."

"Have you ever worn zebra stripes?"

"No, nor any other kind of animal stripes."

"I think zebra stripes might look good on you with your blond hair."

Sally shook her head and took another bite of her steak.

"Do you wear red?"

"Yes, of course, though I favor blue."

"I guess that would look good on you."

"Thank you, but my appearance isn't terribly important in my job."

"Really? Granddad says an attractive salesperson will sell more than an unattractive salesperson."

"So he only hires beautiful people?"

"No, he only hires people who present an attractive picture, whether they are beautiful or not."

"I think a person's smile is the most important thing."

"Yeah, I guess that counts, too."

They finished their meal and did the dishes together, though Sally teased Hunter about his lack of experience with the dishes.

"Now shall we have coffee by the fire?" he asked.

"Of course. Let me fix a tray."

They settled on the sofa, in front of the fire that had died down to glowing coals. Sally poured the coffee and they both sipped it slowly. Finally, with no conversation, Sally closed her eyes for just a moment.

When she next opened her eyes, it was almost nine in the morning, and Hunter Bedford was sleeping next to her.

CHAPTER FIVE

"HUNTER!"

Sally was practically screaming as she stared at her watch.

He slowly came awake. "What's the matter?" he asked groggily.

"Hunter, it's after nine o'clock! You stayed here all night!"

"I did? I'm sorry, Sally. I just closed my eyes for a minute because—because I was so tired. I didn't intend to stay so long."

He didn't sound at all upset. Sally closed her eyes again. All she could think about was what people would say. "Hunter, you don't understand. In a small town, any kind of behavior like this will cause all kinds of talk. You've got to leave as quickly and as quietly as possible."

"Sure. I'll slip out, but it's no big deal, Sally."

"Maybe not in Denver, but here it is. Please, just go and don't say anything to anyone."

"No, I won't."

He crossed to the front door, picking up his coat and putting it on. Then he opened the front door and came to a complete stop as snow blew into his face.

"Close the door!" Sally yelled, even as she ran for the mop.

He did as she asked, but he just stood there, with snow all over him.

She returned with the mop and handed him a towel, telling him to wipe himself off. Then she began mopping the entryway.

"Uh, Sally, I thought you wanted me to leave."

"Not in a snowstorm, Hunter. I'd forgotten about the storm coming. I guess it's still out there."

"Yeah," he said as he wiped himself dry. "What do we do now?"

How she wished for her parents at that moment. There wouldn't be a problem if she had them here. With a sigh, she said, "We go to the kitchen and make breakfast."

Hunter followed her, offering to cook for her again.

"No, I think I'll cook this morning. It won't take long."

She began by putting bacon on to cook, mixing eggs in a bowl and adding milk, and buttering bread to go in the oven. Hunter took over that chore, buttering four pieces of bread. He also poured some juice for the two of them. In between the cooking, Sally cleaned out the coffeepot and refilled it. By the time she served the eggs and bacon and Hunter served the toast, the coffee was perking.

"This is a great breakfast, Sally," Hunter said as he ate.

"I'm glad you're enjoying it," she said politely, but she kept looking out of the window at the near blizzard. In a way she was grateful for the storm because it might allow her to get Hunter out of her house before someone saw him.

He got up and poured two cups of coffee once the coffeepot finished.

"Thank you," she said and took a sip of coffee.

"No sugar or milk for you?"

"No, I take mine black. Do you need something for your coffee?"

"I could use a little milk. I like it in my coffee in the mornings."

Sally got up and poured some milk in a small pitcher and put it on the table next to Hunter. Then she sat down again.

"How long will it last?"

"What?" she asked, looking at him. She knew he'd said something, but she'd been thinking about her dilemma.

"I asked how long the storm will last."

"I don't know. We'll turn on the television and listen to the weather." There was a small television on the kitchen cabinet and Sally switched it on and then sat back down. The picture was of a weather map and the man was explaining that the snowstorm should ease up early in the afternoon.

"There's your answer."

"Are you going to let me stay here until it eases up, as the man said?" Hunter asked.

"Of course. There's not much else that we can do," Sally said, but secretly she wished she wasn't snowbound with this particular man right now.

They finished their breakfast in silence. After cleaning the kitchen, they both stared at each other.

"What do we do now?" Hunter asked.

"We just have to wait. Do you like to read? I've got some murder mysteries, some romance novels, some true crime books. Or we have some movies we could watch."

"If you don't mind, I'd like to look at the mysteries. I enjoy those."

"Of course. Come this way." She led him into the living room where one end of the area was bookshelves. She pointed out the mysteries, her dad's favorites, and told him to choose any of them to read. Once he found one of his favorite authors on the shelf, he settled down with the newest book.

"I'll be back in a minute," she said and slipped from the room. She went upstairs to her room and took out fresh clothes to change into. She looked longingly at her shower, but she didn't think that would be wise. Once she'd changed into fresh clothes she felt much better.

Then she walked into her parents' room and found some old jeans her dad had owned when he was young. He'd kept one pair, saying he intended to lose weight one day and he wanted to be sure he reached the right size. She thought that pair of jeans would fit Hunter. Then she un-wrapped a shirt she'd bought her dad the last time she had been in Denver. She held it for a moment in her hands and thought about how her dad would have looked in it. Fortunately no one in Bailey would've seen her dad wearing it so there wouldn't be any questions asked when Hunter was suddenly spotted in it. She took both items downstairs to Hunter and told him to take the clothes to the bathroom and see if they fit.

A few minutes later, he came back into the room, looking like the clothes had been made for him. The only problem now was his feet. The loafers he was wearing weren't appropriate for the snowstorm outside and he would definitely need some sturdier shoes. "What size shoe do you wear?" Sally asked.

"Elevens," Hunter said with a shrug.

"Just a minute." Her dad wore eleven-and-a-halfs, so he should be able to wear her dad's boots. They were actually hiking boots, but her father always wore them in the winter. Sally brought a pair into the room with clean socks. And soon he was fully outfitted. "Sally, this is great. Thanks. I was feeling a little grubby this morning."

"Dad has—had an electric shaver if you want to use it. I believe it's still upstairs. I'll go get it."

Once he had shaved, Hunter felt much better and he again settled down with the mystery, perfectly happy.

About one o'clock, the storm was just beginning to subside. Sally went into the kitchen and made some turkey sandwiches and called Hunter to lunch. He put aside his book, which he'd read halfway through, and came into the kitchen.

"This looks good, Sally. Thanks."

"No problem. We'll be able to get out soon. I didn't want you starving for lunch."

"This book is really good. I'd read some of this guy's earlier books, but I think this is the best one I've read."

"Yes, my dad really liked him. He always said the more he wrote the better he'd be."

"So your dad read a lot?"

"Yes. He always preferred reading to movies."

"Hmm, which do you prefer?"

"Both. I used to watch movies with my mom, but then got my love of reading from my dad."

"Watching movies is something to be shared, isn't it?"

"Yes. Mom and I would start crying at almost the same time and Dad would always tease us about watching the weepies as he called them."

"Yeah. I try not to watch those kinds of movies. I'd rather people not see me cry."

Sally just smiled and took a bite of sandwich. A few minutes later, after they'd cleaned up the lunch dishes, Sally decided she could make it across to the store.

"I'm going to the store. You can go to your place, if you want. I won't expect you to work today."

"Don't be silly. I don't think it's safe for you to be there alone. I'm ready to help you."

"I'll be fine."

"No. I'll come with you. After all, I'm dressed in different clothes. No one will realize I spent the night here."

"I hope not."

She put on her coat and wrapped a scarf around her hair and her neck, pulled on gloves and opened the door. The wind was still blowing, but not as hard as before. Only a few snowflakes were dashing around.

They walked in snow about six inches deep across the street to the store. Sally unlocked the back door and stepped inside, making room for Hunter. Then she relocked the back door.

"I have to straighten the store first of all, in case we have any customers," she explained.

Hunter nodded and followed her into the main store. "I'll take the men's departments and you take the ladies'," he suggested and went to the area he'd chosen and began to work.

Sally watched him go. He was certainly being coopera-
tive and she thought back to the conversation they'd had last
night about her selling the store. Although they'd overcome
their argument Sally still felt a little nervous at the thought
of Hunter only being nice to her to get his hands on her
store. The thought made her shudder.

Moving to the ladies' departments, she hurriedly
straightened the goods, making them look neat and ready
for customers.

When they had both finished those jobs, Sally brought
out the huge box of holiday decorations for the store. They
hadn't had any customers at all so Sally thought it would
be a good idea to make the most of the quiet spell and
decorate the store. She told Hunter her idea. "First, we
have to trim both windows with these artificial strips of
greenery. Then we'll hang ornaments on them."

"How do we attach it to the wall?"

"Dad put up hooks that we can use. It makes it very
easy." She stepped into the window and began attaching the
greenery to the hooks.

"Nice job. It certainly makes it an easy job, doesn't it?"

"Yes. Dad loved efficiency." She kept her face turned.
Thinking about her dad decorating the windows wasn't
easy for her and reminded her that he had really gone.
Once she had the greenery in place in her window, she
began attaching Christmas balls to hang down.

"Hunter? Have you—oh, very nice. Well, we both
finished that task very quickly. Now we have two wreaths
to put on the front door." She opened the doors and took
one wreath and hung it. Hunter did the other one.

They reclosed the doors, glad to shut out the cold air. "What's next?"

"Well, we put up an artificial tree. It's in the storeroom."

Hunter volunteered to go fetch it. In the meantime, Sally cleared a space. When Hunter brought it in, they put it up together. It was a prelit tree, which made decorating it easier. They attached the ornaments and put a star on top.

"Hey, I'm beginning to feel all Christmassy," Hunter said with a grin.

"I know. It's hard not to, with all this."

He gave her a quick look. "Does it bring back memories?"

"Yes. Dad always made it so much fun to decorate for Christmas," Sally said, sniffing a little.

"Sorry it's so hard, Sally. But it will get easier."

"Yes, I know. Now I need to go put on the Christmas music that Dad always played."

"What was his favorite Christmas music?"

Sally couldn't hold back a smile. "Bing Crosby's 'White Christmas.' It's appropriate today, isn't it?"

"That it is," he said, a smile on his face.

Sally was struck again by Hunter's attractive appearance. As the expression went, he'd be able to sell refrigerators to Eskimos.

She hurried to the back room and put on the music they played every Christmas. Just as the music started up, she heard the bell over the front door sound. Rushing back into the store, she discovered a family taking off their outer wraps.

"Mrs Denton, how are you feeling?" she asked. Sally had heard last week that Mrs Denton had been suffering from a bad cold.

"I'm fine, but don't get close to Harry," she said, motioning to her husband. "He's not doing so well."

"Ah, it's one of those things you pass around?"

"I'm afraid so, but he refused to stay at home."

"Well, a family shopping trip may be just what he needs. So you want some help, or do you just want to wander?"

"We'll just wander. The kids were anxious to come. Lots of pent-up energy from this morning."

"Of course. Let us know if you need us."

Sally motioned to Hunter and went to the back room. "We need these wreaths hung up at intervals around the store. Wherever there is space."

He took the stack of smaller wreaths and went out into the store. Sally looked around, trying to remember what else they did for Christmas. But she couldn't think of anything.

Donations for the Christmas Festival had been trickling in slowly and were beginning to pile up in the back room. Sally started going through the clothing articles to see if they were in decent shape. She found some that needed minor repairs and she put them in a separate pile. Others were in beautiful shape. She hung them up on a clothing rack, one for men and one for ladies.

"Sally? What else do I need to do?"

"I think that's everything, Hunter. If you could keep an eye on the store while I sort these donations, I'd appreciate it."

"I'll be glad to."

It was a relief for Sally to know that someone else was doing some of the things on her list. Cutting the jobs in half left her a little time to do other things. She found herself singing along to the Christmas music, in a much better mood.

* * *

Hunter kept an eye on the customers, and tidied up the check-out area at the same time. More and more customers arrived, much to his surprise.

He finally had to disturb Sally and get her to come out and help him. When Mary and Ethel arrived, Sally slipped over to the house to make sandwiches for her and Hunter when they had time to eat, which, unfortunately, wasn't until after seven.

They kept the store open until eight and then Sally locked the front door and let the customers out as they finished their shopping.

When the last shopper had gone, Mary and Ethel had already finished cleaning the dressing rooms and straightening up the store. Sally wearily thanked them and let them out the front door. Then she looked for Hunter. She finally found him straightening the wrapping paper behind the counter.

"Hunter, it's time to go home. It's been a long day."

"Yes, it has," he agreed, standing and stretching. "But you did a lot of business this afternoon."

"Yes, we did. Thanks for helping out."

"My pleasure, that's what I'm here for."

Earlier in the day she'd counted out the money she owed Mary and Ethel and had included money for Hunter. "Here's your pay," she said.

"What?" he asked, staring at the envelope she was handing him.

"I told you I'd pay you what I pay Mary and Ethel. It isn't a lot but you've certainly earned it."

"I'm not taking your money, Sally."

"Hunter, I insist."

"Give it to charity. You're doing me a favor."

"No, I—"

He bent over and kissed her. "There. I'm going to do that every time you argue with me about it. I'm not taking it."

"But—"

He kissed her again, hoping she continued to argue with him. He was enjoying those kisses.

"You—you can't do that, Hunter."

"What?"

"Kiss me. That's not proper."

"It feels pretty proper to me."

Sally stood there, saying nothing.

Hunter waited, hoping she'd argue with him again.

But she didn't. "Very well. I'll contribute it to the funds we take on the night of the Festival, if you insist."

"I do," he said solemnly, wishing she hadn't caved in so quickly.

"Then goodnight."

"Shall I go out the back door? Then I can be sure you make it to your house okay. It's quite dark outside."

"No. I'll be fine."

"Sally, I think I should go out the back with you. It would be dangerous for you to go alone. I insist."

"Why do you get to argue and I don't?" she demanded.

A rueful grin appeared on his face. "That's just the way things work, honey. Though you could kiss me, if you want."

"No, thank you." She put on her coat and scarf and gathered up the keys and some of the garments that needed repair. Then she went to the door, not looking to see if he was following.

But he was right behind her, holding the door as she walked through.

She locked the door after he stepped out. The only light was a small light above the store door. The area around them was pitch-black.

"We should've left the front porch light on," Hunter muttered.

"No, I never do that. It would burn all day for nothing."

"I think that's okay if it's on when you come out. It would provide some safety."

"I'll be fine."

"I think you're arguing with me again," he said, leaning toward her.

She turned away. "No, I'm not. Will you be all right making your way to the bed-and-breakfast?"

"Yes. These boots are great. The snow doesn't get in."

"Okay, well I'll see you Monday then."

"Wait, what are you doing tomorrow?"

Sally looked at him, a puzzled expression on her face. "What?"

"What do you do on Sunday?"

"I usually go to church, but I may not in the morning. I'm very tired. I'll probably sleep in and then work on these garments to get them ready for the Festival."

"Ah. I was just wondering. I'll see you," he said and turned to walk away. As soon as he'd convinced her he was leaving, he slowed down until she was in her house. Then he tromped along the snow-covered street until he reached his bed-and-breakfast. But he wished he'd been able to go home with Sally.

* * *

Sally did as she'd told Hunter. She slept in, to recuperate from the hard day on Saturday. Then she got up and ate some oatmeal, her usual fare. After that, with the television on for entertainment, she began repairing the garments that had been donated for the Christmas Festival.

Though she seemed happy and comfortable, Sally wasn't really. She kept listening for sounds from her parents. They usually accompanied her wherever she went in the house. But now there were no sounds. No one moving around, no one talking. Just the television.

She was feeling the loneliness again, as she had since her parents' deaths. So what was making it so different today? The answer struck her, but she didn't want to admit it. Finally she had to realize that Hunter being in the house with her yesterday had made a difference.

Now she was alone again.

Shifting in her chair, she tried to tell herself she'd get used to being alone. Just be patient.

She certainly hoped so. She didn't want to remember Hunter's voice, his soft kisses because she'd argued with him. Those kisses in particular. They had no place in her memories.

But they did.

She was remembering how Hunter had moved around the kitchen, talking, laughing, arguing. And she even thought she could still smell him, a nice masculine smell.

A loud knock on her front door disturbed her thoughts.

CHAPTER SIX

SHE regretted the fact that her father had never put in a peephole so she could determine who was at her door. It had never seemed necessary before, but now, by herself, she found she'd like to know who was at her door before she opened it.

Pausing, she called out, "Who is it?"

"Sally? It's me, Hunter."

She was at war with her feelings. She wanted desperately to open the door, but her better judgment told her not to. What could Hunter want on a Sunday? She thought that maybe it was something to do with the store; she hoped so and finally, she opened the door.

"Hi," she said, offering a tentative smile.

"May I come in? It's still cold out here."

She moved back. "Yes, of course."

"Thanks. How are you doing?"

"Fine. And you?"

"I'm a little bored in my room. I wondered if I could come over and read the mystery you loaned me yesterday. I'm really wrapped up in the story."

Normally she would tell him to take the book with him,

but it was one her dad had chosen himself. She didn't want to give up anything of her dad's just yet. "Yes, I guess so, if you don't mind reading it here. I'd like to keep track of Dad's things."

"Yeah, I thought you might feel that way."

"I'll get the book down for you. Take off your coat and get comfortable."

"Thanks, Sally. I'll try to stay out of your way."

She didn't say anything, but Hunter Bedford would stand out wherever he found himself. In her house, lonely as it was, she certainly couldn't ignore him. After he settled in a chair with the book, she knelt down and started a fire in the fireplace.

As the fire caught hold, Hunter looked up. "Nice, thanks, Sally."

She nodded and then returned to the kitchen. She'd gone from sewing to mixing up some dough to make gingerbread men that she served to kids when they came in the store.

There was only one week left until the Christmas Festival. Penny would be sending the Christmas tree soon and she and Hunter would decorate it on Thursday and Friday. Sally had arranged for Mary's teenage daughter to come and help in the store next week until Christmas Eve, when they would close at four.

Sally knew that she might need to excuse Hunter on Christmas Eve, since he would have to drive to Denver for the holiday. They could manage on their own. But the sadness she felt at him leaving couldn't be done away with.

Suddenly the kitchen door swung open and Hunter was standing there. "What is it I'm smelling?" he asked.

"I'm making gingerbread men," she said. She'd just emptied the big mixing bowl on wax paper on the kitchen table and was ready to roll out the dough.

"Can I help?"

"Maybe. You could cut them out while I put them on the baking pans, if you want."

"I'll try."

She handed him two cookie cutters shaped like gingerbread men.

"These are little, aren't they?"

"Yeah, I know. But these are cookies I hand out to the kids that come in with their parents."

"Oh. I see. Yes, that size makes sense."

He waited as she rolled out the dough. Then he began cutting out the cookies. Sally watched as he cut the cookies as close to each other as possible, thereby conserving dough. She began putting them on the cookie trays. As soon as she had one filled, she put it in the oven and set the timer. Then she started on the next tray. They worked well together and had soon made a hundred and forty-four cookies.

"Hey, they turned out great!" Hunter said.

"Oh, we're not through with them yet," Sally said with a smile. She took white icing and mixed some with blue, some with red, and some with green. She filled three decorating funnels with each color. Then she decorated a cookie, using the blue for the eyes, a curved red line for its mouth and three green buttons down its middle. "See?"

"He looks terrific."

"So, I'll do his face and you do the buttons. Okay?"

"Absolutely. I haven't had this much fun in years. My grandmother would've liked this tradition."

"Did she do a lot of baking?"

"Yeah. She'd start a couple of weeks before Christmas, with cookies and then she'd bake cakes and then lastly pies."

"Wow! You must've eaten a lot of sweets!"

"No, she gave a lot of them away actually."

"That's lovely."

"Yeah. When she died, so many people came to her funeral, telling us how much they'd miss getting those sweet gifts at Christmas time."

Sally sighed, thinking about things she'd miss that her mother and father always did.

"Damn! I did it again, didn't I?" When she sent him a quizzical look, he said, "I made you think about your parents dying."

"Yes, but it felt good, knowing they'd be missed for good reasons."

"Good, I'm glad," Hunter said and smiled.

When they finished all the cookies, Sally stacked them in a big box to take to the store the next morning. Then she took out some chicken and put it in the oven to bake. "Would you like to stay for dinner, Hunter?" She had enjoyed the afternoon so much she didn't see any reason why she shouldn't extend their evening.

"I'd be delighted, Sally. You're such a good cook."

Sally laughed at Hunter's compliment. "I don't think you've eaten much of my cooking before, except for break-fast. We ate your cooking for dinner, remember?"

"Ah, but I did try one gingerbread man. He's the best I've ever had."

Sally chuckled. "You're easy!"

"Am not! I have absolutely high standards, taught to me by my grandmother."

"Very well. We'll see what you think about my chicken."

"What else are we having?"

"Mashed potatoes and green beans, plus rolls, of course."

"Sounds good. What can I do?"

"Peel potatoes?"

"Sure. I can't mess up too much with that."

While Hunter peeled the potatoes, Sally put on the green beans on low heat. Then she put the rolls on a cookie sheet and buttered them on top. Then she made iced tea.

After she set the table, she put the potatoes on to boil. Then she fixed the coffeepot for after dinner. In less than half an hour, they had dinner ready.

"Man, it smells good," he said as he sat down.

"I'm glad you think so."

She passed him the chicken and he took several pieces. "This is so tender," he said after taking a bite.

"I know, my mom taught me this recipe."

"She was obviously a very good cook, too."

"Yes," Sally said with a sigh. "Fortunately she taught me all of her recipes. We took turns cooking."

"I can see why she wanted you to stay at home after college."

Sally smiled. "Oh, you didn't get out of work when you weren't cooking, it was your job to do the dishes, but you had to do one or the other."

"And what did your dad do?"

"The store books. He brought them here to the kitchen and did them while whoever cooked worked alongside him. Then, after dinner, he'd finish them, so we were ready to go the next morning."

"No wonder you're worn-out. You've got too much to do, trying to do the cooking, cleaning and the books each night."

"I'll get better at managing. It will just take a while."

"It sounds like you had some happy times with your family here, Sally. I like that," Hunter said as he looked at her fondly.

They ate in silence for several minutes. Then Sally looked at Hunter. "Do you want to have a family?"

"Yeah. Someday. I have to settle down first, figure out what I'm doing with my life."

"Aren't you going to work for your granddad?" she asked in surprise.

He didn't answer for several minutes. Then he looked up. "I don't know. I've tried it, but he wants me to work in the corporate offices and I like working in the store. You know, meeting people, placing orders, tidying up. The things you do every day."

"Oh. And does that disappoint your grandfather?"

"Yeah. He's got a great guy working in the corporate offices and I've told him to make the guy his second-in-command instead of me. So far, he won't listen to me."

"But surely you wouldn't be happy just working in the store. I don't think salespeople make that much money."

"Grandmother left me quite a bit of money. I've invested it and receive interest each year. I'd be fine."

"I see."

"You don't believe me?"

"Yes, I believe you, but I can't help thinking about your poor grandfather. You're the only one he has to leave his estate to, to carry on."

"But I need to be happy, Sally," he said and as he looked her in her eyes Sally could sense the trouble that this issue had caused him.

"Yes, of course, but don't you think you owe your grandfather some loyalty?"

"I'll always love him and do anything I can to make him happy…except sacrifice my happiness."

"But—"

"No, Sally. If you had had a dream to go to the big city and work, would your parents have insisted you stay here?"

"No, of course not, but—"

"They were lucky that you loved your home and your family job."

"Maybe."

"I promised I'd stay, but I've tried the corporate life. I find it so boring, so stressful, so—so irritating. I can't see myself doing that the rest of my life."

Sally placed her hand on Hunter's arm and looked at him, an understanding in her eyes. "I know how you feel. I just hope you can make your grandfather see that."

"I've tried to explain it to him over and over again. He loves the grand scheme of owning a store. I love the little things about owning a store. It's just totally different."

Sally thought he sounded perfect for her store, as her partner, but she wasn't about to suggest such a thing. That role would be for her husband, and Hunter didn't want to marry her, of course. He would marry a smart city girl rather than a small town girl like her.

They cleaned the kitchen together and Sally prepared a tray for the coffee. Then she led the way into the living room.

"Just promise me one thing, Hunter."

"What's that, Sally?"

"That you go home by nine o'clock. No going to sleep on the sofa all night."

"I promise. But I think we got away with it. Which reminds me. I need to leave the snow boots here. I can wear my loafers home."

"You can take your loafers with you, but you might as well keep the snow boots. Dad's not going to wear them again."

"Thanks, Sally. I appreciate that."

She poured him a cup of coffee and passed it to him. Then she poured herself a cup. It was decaf, because she didn't want anything to keep her awake. But she'd be sure to send him home before she closed her eyes again.

Monday morning, Mary's daughter came into the store to work with her mother during Christmas vacation. Susie was immediately attracted to Hunter, and Sally stiffened when she saw the young lady trailing him around the store.

She immediately asked Susie to assist a woman with two little children. That would keep her busy. Hunter sent Sally a smile of relief and Sally returned the smile, but she hoped he didn't think her actions were anything other than keeping Susie away from him. Sally would have to keep an eye on her.

For the moment, however, Susie was occupied with a demanding customer. So Sally went to the back room where she began sorting through yet more things that had been donated for the Festival. As she went through the items she began to think about her Sunday, with Hunter visiting her. His presence in her house had made a difference and it made Sally feel warm to think about it again now.

"Oh, I forgot!" She hurried out into the store with the gingerbread cookies. She offered cookies to the children Susie was helping. The mother was grateful as it occupied the children's minds so their mother could shop. Sally found several other children and offered them a gingerbread man, too.

Hunter saw her and nodded with a smile. He knew that he'd done his share in creating the gingerbread men. His next customer had several children with him and Hunter immediately came over to get gingerbread men for his little customers.

"Are you managing all right?" Sally asked in a whisper.

"Yeah, as long as Susie is occupied. I don't need her following me everywhere," Hunter said, frowning.

"If I don't see her, just tell her mother. She'll take care of it."

"We'll see," Hunter said, not promising anything.

Sally didn't say anything else. As she turned to go to the back room again, however, Hunter asked, "What are your plans for dinner?"

"My plans?" she asked in surprise.

"Yeah, I thought I'd take you out to repay you for dinner last night."

"That's not necessary, Hunter. It was no big deal."

"Yes, it was. And you know I don't like to eat alone."

"I didn't mean to be rude, Hunter, but I don't think having dinner together would be a good idea."

"Why not?"

"It's a small town, Hunter. People are already speculating about you. If I have dinner with you again, romance rumors will fly all over town."

"What's so wrong with that?"

"Well, nothing at the moment, but what about when you leave? If people think that I've fallen in love with you, they'll all feel sorry for me, sure you've broken my heart. I'd rather avoid that kind of gossip, thank you very much."

"Surely we can eat together without starting all those rumors."

"The only way is if we make it clear that there is nothing going on between us and I pay for my own dinner."

"That's silly, Sally! You fed me last night, I should be able to return the favor!"

"Yes, I know, but I don't want to advertise the fact that you have been having late night dinners at my place, either, Hunter. Do you see?"

He stood there staring at her, his hands on his hips. Then he said, "Okay. We go Dutch. Right?"

"Yes, but we won't be able to go until after eight, when the store closes."

"Will the restaurant still be open then?"

"Yes, they're open until nine."

"Good. Then we'll close the store and go eat dinner, Dutch treat, after we lock up."

"Fine." Somehow, hearing his words, as if they always did things together, warmed her cold heart. But she had to remember that Hunter would be leaving very soon and she would be back to being on her own again.

When the day came to a close at eight o'clock, Sally was tired. She would have preferred to have gone home and had a bowl of soup and an early night. But Hunter was joining her for dinner at the Diamond Back. After Mary, Susie and Ethel had left, she gathered her purse and coat and located Hunter still straightening things in the men's department. "Hunter? Leave that until the morning."

"Okay. I'm starving. Are you?"

"Yes. It's been a long day."

"And a busy one. Is business better this Christmas than before?"

"Maybe a little. We always do a lot of business at Christmas time."

"I can believe it. Your store is always so welcoming. Especially with the Christmas music."

"Surely your stores play Christmas music during the holidays, too," Sally said as she walked down the sidewalk.

"Yes, but it's drowned out by the crowds and the traffic outside. It's just different here in Bailey."

"True. We don't have traffic jams here."

Hunter put his hand on her back as they began to cross the street. Sally could feel his big hand as it pressed against her spine and she felt a tingle of electricity trace its way up to her neck. She shivered and pulled her coat closer around her, sure that it was just the cold causing her to shiver.

"Don't do that, Hunter," Sally said and began to walk faster.

"What's wrong?"

"You mustn't act like we're on a date! We're just friends, remember, business acquaintances."

"You mean because I put my hand on your back? That's no big deal, honey. I just wanted to be sure you were all right crossing the street. That's all."

"That's not all. It makes it look like we're on a date! And we're not!"

"Right. We're just friends. But I don't let my friends fall on their faces. Even if I'm not dating them."

They reached the restaurant. Hunter reached out to open the door for her. She walked through, but she wasn't happy.

"Sally! How lovely to see you. How's—oh, I didn't realize Mr Bedford was with you. Hello, welcome to our restaurant again, Mr Bedford."

"We thought we'd get a bite to eat after working through supper, Diane. It's not too late, is it?" Sally asked, trying to sound casual.

"Of course not! There's plenty of time. Come right this way." The hostess showed them to the same table they'd occupied before.

Hunter held the chair for Sally, and she sat down. She knew it wouldn't do any good to complain while Diane was there.

Hunter moved around the small table to sit down opposite her.

"Your waitress will be right with you." Diane hurried away, back to her place near the door.

"Don't complain, Sally. I know you think I shouldn't

have pulled your chair out for you, but I promise I'd do that for a friend as well as a date."

"I wasn't going to complain," she lied.

"Good."

She opened her menu and studied the offerings. When the waitress who had served them last time came to their table, she focused on Hunter, just as Susie had.

"Have you made your choices?" she asked breathlessly.

"Yes, I have," Sally said. "I'll have the enchiladas, please, with iced tea."

"I'll have the same," Hunter said easily, smiling at the waitress.

"Yes, sir," Gretchen said as she took the menus and left the table.

"You like Mexican food?" Sally asked, staring at him.

"Yes, I do. I hope it's good."

"It usually is."

When Gretchen brought their iced teas, Sally decided she would make it clear to everyone that she was not on a date with Hunter Bedford. "Oh, Gretchen, do you think that you could make us up separate checks, please. I'll be paying for my own meal this evening."

Gretchen stared at her, clearly not understanding what was happening between these two.

"She's joking, Gretchen," Hunter said. "Just ignore her and bring me the check."

Sally turned to stare at Hunter, unable to believe his betrayal and was about to protest when Gretchen spoke.

"Okay, I will," Gretchen said with a smile for Hunter and left the table.

"Why did you say that, Hunter?" Sally demanded.

"Because I intended to pay for dinner whether you liked it or not. After all, you fed me last night."

"But I told you that I wanted to pay my share of the bill."

"Look, Sally, you can pay me back once we leave the restaurant, if you want, but it's not necessary. It's a blow to my masculinity if you pay for your meal."

Sally held her head in her hands. She hadn't imagined the evening would turn out like this. She lifted her head and could already see Gretchen whispering to Diane and looking over in their direction. Sally groaned, "But you don't understand small towns, Hunter. By now, half the town will think I'm in love with you!"

CHAPTER SEVEN

"DO THEY think you're in love with anyone else you have dinner with?" Hunter asked in exasperation.

"That's just it. I don't have dinner with anyone else. At least, not usually," Sally explained. "There aren't a lot of single men who hang around town."

"Then how do you expect to find someone to marry?" he demanded, anger building in him. "How do you even find out what kind of man you like?"

They were interrupted then as Gretchen returned with their dinner. Sally thanked her, not showing any signs of the anger she was feeling towards Hunter. Once Gretchen had moved away, Sally turned back to her dinner companion. "I did date some men in college, Hunter. Certainly not many, but enough to know what kind of man I'm looking for."

"How old are you now, Sally?" Hunter asked sharply.

"I'm twenty-five, soon to be twenty-six," she told him, raising her chin.

"So you haven't dated in at least three years? That's crazy, Sally! Surely you must be really lonely."

Sally thought back to how lonely it had been since her parents' deaths and had to admit that Hunter's presence had certainly changed that, but there was no way she was going to admit that to him now. Instead she said stubbornly, "Hunter, I'm so busy with the store since Mom and Dad died that I don't have time to be lonely."

"Right. I'm sorry, but—never mind. Just enjoy your dinner."

He bent over his food, not looking at her. After a few minutes' silence, Sally said, "You handled that man well who came in by himself today. I don't know who he is, but you obviously made him feel very welcome."

Hunter looked at her for a moment, clearly pleased that their little dispute was over. "He's here visiting relatives. He wanted to get each of them a gift."

"That was nice of him. Did you have to wrap all of his choices?"

"Mary did it, actually. I'm not as good in that department as I should be." Hunter smiled.

"That's the thing about small towns. Here, you have to be a jack-of-all-trades. We are the gift wrap department if it's needed."

"That's what I like about your store. You're involved in every aspect, and you know if there's a problem at once."

"Yes," Sally said with a sigh. "Last year, the furnace went out. We knew about it at once, but we couldn't get a repairman here for three days."

"What did your dad do?"

"He tried to fix it himself, but that didn't work. All he could do was harass the company until they got someone up here to fix it. Oh, and pay extra for their speed," she said with a laugh.

"So he closed the store for three days?"

"Oh, no. We all just bundled up and he brought in a couple of space heaters. We all tried to stay close to them."

"I can imagine. I'm glad we haven't had that problem this winter."

"Definitely not." She took a bite of her enchiladas. "Is your food good?"

"Delicious. It was a good choice."

They ate in silence for a moment longer and Sally thought how pleasant it was to share a meal with Hunter. Even though they had their disagreements she was surprised at how easily they got on with each other.

Hunter took a long drink of his iced tea before he spoke. "Say, if I am going to play Santa at the Festival this year am I still going out there to see the children all by myself?"

Sally looked down at her meal. "I don't see why not. It shouldn't be a problem, should it?"

"Yeah, I think it will be a problem. I think I'm going to need a Santa's helper. I think you should come out there with me."

"But we've never had a Santa's helper before, Hunter."

"So, start a new tradition this year. That way you get to share in the experience, too. Come on, Sally, we talked about this before and you said you'd think about it," Hunter said, smiling mischievously.

"I don't know," Sally said, her forehead wrinkling as she

thought about his suggestion. She liked the idea of starting a new tradition and maybe it would help her feel more involved, especially since her mom and dad wouldn't be there.

"Come on, Sally. It would be fun."

"I'll think about it. I really will, this time. I promise."

They resumed their eating, continuing to talk about their day in the store. When they'd both finished their meal, Hunter took the check and paid Diane, thanking her for a good meal, and they went back out in the cold.

"You know, when you're inside, you forget how cold it is out here." His breath stood out in the night air.

"I know. It's always a shock."

When they'd crossed the street, she paused. "Thank you for dinner, even though I should've paid for my meal. It was a fun night."

"Yeah, it was, but why does the evening have to end here?"

"Because this is where we split up. Your bed-and-break-fast is in the opposite direction from my house."

"It's not far. I'll see you home first."

"Hunter, I'll be all right. After all, I know everyone here in Bailey."

"That may be so, but I don't like the idea of you going home by yourself. I'll see you to your door and then I'll go back to the bed-and-breakfast."

Though she huffed several times, she couldn't dissuade Hunter from his self-appointed task of seeing her home. Secretly Sally had to admit that she liked the fact that Hunter had walked her home. He was certainly a gentle-man. She began walking faster, not to get away from him this time, but because it had turned colder this evening.

"You don't have to run, Sally. I'm not going to give up you know!"

"I know, but it's so cold out here."

"That's true. Look, we're almost there already. That's something else I like about Bailey. It doesn't take so long to get anywhere. Well, here we are."

Sally stopped; the quick walk home had made her a little breathless and her cheeks were a nice rosy-red. "Thank you for walking me home, Hunter."

"You know what, Sally? I'm glad I paid for your dinner, because I think this did turn into a date." And, without warning, he pulled her into his arms and kissed her, a deeper kiss than he'd ever given her before.

It took her a minute before she realized what was happening. She'd been taken by surprise by his kiss, she told herself. That was the only thing that could explain that momentary pause when she had enjoyed his kiss, the feel of his lips on her own. "Hunter! You—you shouldn't have done that." She said now, stuttering slightly with the shock.

"I think I should've done that the first day. Then I would have a lot more kisses under my belt." He whispered good night and stepped off the porch. But he didn't walk away. Instead he just stood there staring at her.

"What are you waiting for?"

"For you to go in and lock up. I want to know you're safe before I leave."

"Of course I'm safe!"

"Then go inside and lock the door. When you do, I'll head back to the bed-and-breakfast."

"Ooh! Good night!" She entered the house and slammed the door.

With a gentle smile on his lips, he moved down the quiet street through the snow that had begun to melt that day, though it wasn't all gone. He'd enjoyed his dinner with Sally. She was an enjoyable companion.

The next morning, Sally went in to work early to place some orders on the computer. They were running low on some of their goods and she wanted to get more in before the Festival. She let Billy in at eight-fifteen. That was when he usually got there, willing to wait out in the cold if Sally hadn't arrived.

A few minutes later, they both heard a knock on the front door.

"Oh! That's probably Hunter. Will you go let him in, please, Billy?"

"Okay, Sally."

Hunter came into the break room shortly after, still wrapped in his outer coat. "Good morning, Sally. It sure is cold out there today."

"Yes, it is. Good morning, Hunter."

"What are you doing?"

"Restocking. We're running a little low on some of our items."

"Yeah, I noticed that, too. Do you have the men's department covered?"

"No, I'd totally forgotten that. What do we need there?" she asked in surprise. Sally hadn't realized how much she had relied on Hunter over the last few days. He had practically managed the men's department single-handedly.

He named off four items and she hurriedly added them to the list. "Thanks, Hunter. Is there anything else you can think of that we need?"

"More wrapping paper? If it's going to get busier, it seems to me that we'll need more paper."

"And bows. Good thinking."

Once that was done, she shut down the computer and went out in the store to check its appearance. Several areas needed straightening and she and Hunter split them up and quickly had the store in perfect condition. Of course, once the shoppers came in, it wouldn't stay that way, but that was the nature of the beast.

When the grandfather clock in the store rang nine o'clock, Sally unlocked the front door. Another day began. They were quite busy most of the day, but there were times when they took breaks. Sally didn't mention the word dinner to anyone, especially Hunter. She didn't intend to find herself in that position again this evening.

When she locked up the store at eight o'clock, Hunter remained behind to walk her home and be sure she locked herself in. She wanted to tell him how much she appreciated that aspect of his presence, but she didn't. She didn't want to admit out loud how hard it was to go out the back door at night and cross the darkened street by herself.

It had never been an issue with her parents there. If she and her mother left a little early, to go home and start dinner, they were together, or all three of them went home together. Now, she was always alone. Except for Hunter. And on Christmas Eve, that would end.

The next day, the stock she'd ordered was delivered.

Billy unpacked them, but it was up to her, Hunter, Mary, Ethel and Susie, to get the items into the store to be sold. They all had to be tagged and appropriately displayed.

Sally worked on that all morning. Everyone else helped customers. Before Sally could finish that, she received a call from her cousin, Penny. After speaking to her for a while and catching up on things, Sally hung up the phone and called Hunter to one side.

"Hunter, my cousin just called and needs eight men's presents in the fifty dollar to seventy-five dollar range. Do you think you could pick some suitable things out for me?"

"Sure. We're not too busy right now. Just gifts for men?" he asked curiously.

"Yes, I should have clarified that for you. These are gifts for the cowboys who work for her on the ranch."

"Cowboys? I'm not sure I know enough about—okay, I guess I can find some."

"Thank you, Hunter. I'm still trying to get the new items ready for sale or I'd help you. But if you'll just bring them to the checkout counter, I'll look at them before I ring them up."

"Okay," he said and walked over to the men's department to begin the search for suitable gifts.

Sally returned to tagging the new items when the phone rang again. "Oh! Yes, thank you. I'll be right out."

She grabbed her coat, spoke briefly to Billy and then told Mary that they'd be outside for a few minutes. Then she, with Billy following, hurried to the town center, a couple of storefronts away. There, on a big truck, lay the town tree. Jake Larson, Penny's manager, and a couple of cowboys were waiting for her instructions.

Billy had brought out the half-barrel they used every year to hold the tree upright. The cowboys, with Billy's help, got the tree in the half-barrel and tied four guidewires to the ground to stabilize it. Then they all gathered in front of the tree to determine if it was straight.

"Thanks, guys. You did a great job picking out the tree."

Jake smiled at her. "Oh, Penny did that. She took a lot of time finding the right one."

"And you froze while she decided?" Sally asked with a grin.

"I didn't mind. She wanted to be sure she found the right one this year."

"Well, you can tell her from me that she definitely did. Thanks again, Jake."

They all said goodbye and Jake and his men got into the truck to go back to the ranch. Billy just stood there, staring up at the tree.

"Are you all right, Billy?" she asked.

"Yeah, I'm okay, Sally. I guess I didn't think we'd have a tree this year. But it looks good, doesn't it? Your daddy would be proud, Sally."

Sally felt the tears threaten at the back of her eyes at Billy's kind words and hugged the man fondly.

"Thanks for your help, Billy."

"Okay," the elderly man said, a little embarrassed at Sally's affectionate hug.

"I'm going back in the store now, Billy, it's cold out here."

"Good idea, let's go." And they both walked back to the store together. Hunter looked up as she came in. "What happened?"

"We put up the tree. Now all we have to do is decorate it. Do you still think you can help out?"

"Of course," Hunter replied. "Is there anything I should know first?"

"Not really, just be sure you wear some warm clothing," Sally answered, recalling how cold it had been outside just now.

"Right."

The weather report last night had said it would be warmer this weekend. That would make the Christmas Festival more enjoyable. With a prayer that things would go well, Sally returned to her tagging.

The next morning, once the store was ready for customers, Sally and Hunter went out to decorate the tree. Mary and Susie had come in earlier this morning so the store wouldn't be left unattended.

"I wish I could help you decorate it," Susie said, breathing heavily in Hunter's direction.

"I think you'll be needed in the store today," Hunter said, though he smiled at the girl.

"But decorating the tree would be so much more fun."

"Not really," Sally said crisply. "Your fingers feel like they'll fall off and you have to climb that high ladder. It's a lot of hard work."

"Oh, but—"

"Come on, Hunter, we have to go now. Billy? Are you ready to bring out the boxes of decorations?"

"You want them now?" Billy called back.

"Yes, please, Billy."

"Okay, Sally."

"Why don't I go help him?" Hunter asked.

"That would be nice. And you need to bring the tall ladder, too," Sally said, again thinking how gentlemanly Hunter was.

Sally went out the front door as customers were coming in. She greeted each of them and explained what she was doing.

"We thought you might not do a tree this year," one man said. "With your parents' deaths and all."

"Yes, we're doing the tree, and the Festival, just as we have in the past."

She didn't know why people thought they weren't going to have the tree and the Festival. If she did nothing else, she would do those two things, because her parents had done them and counted them important to the small town. She wanted people to remember her parents' contributions to their lives.

Billy and Hunter came from around the storefronts to where the tree had been erected. Hunter carried the extension ladder all by himself, while Billy carried a big box. Once Billy set the box down, he turned around and retraced his steps.

"There are two more boxes to come out," Hunter said, a little out of breath as he stood the ladder up.

"Billy will carry them together I'm sure. We'll get started. I think it's safe to lean the ladder against the tree. Do you feel brave enough to climb up to put the star on top?"

He grinned at her. "I don't see anyone else volunteering."

"I will if heights bother you."

"Fortunately they don't. I'll go up. Where is the star?"

"I think it's in this box." She forced the box open and

found the star. Taking it out, she showed Hunter how it attached to the tree. Then she stood back and held her breath as he climbed to the top of the ladder. He had to reach about four more feet from the top of the ladder to attach the star. When he finished and started down, she slowly let her breath out.

"What's next?" he asked when he reached the bottom.

"The lights. I sent Mr Robinson a note yesterday to see if he could make it. We have to make sure that the lights are put up properly—the last thing we want is a fire! Oh, here he is now."

An older man stepped off the sidewalk and walked over to where Sally and Hunter were standing. "So the decorating starts today, does it?"

"It sure does, Mr Robinson. I appreciate your helping us," Sally said, smiling fondly at the gentleman.

"Glad to do it. Who's this young man?"

"This is Hunter Bedford. He's helping me out until Christmas."

Mr Robinson extended his hand to Hunter and he shook it.

"You can call me Ted, if you want," the man said.

"Thanks, Ted. I sure am glad you're here, because I don't know that much about electrical things."

"Not a problem, Hunter. I'll show you a few tricks that I showed Bob. He got right good about things after a while."

Sally smiled ruefully as Ted and Hunter completely left her out as they planned their attack on the tree. In all the years of working with her dad, Mr Robinson had never offered for Sally to call him by his first name.

Billy came out with the other boxes and Sally thanked him and told him to go and get warm back in the store. Then she began laying out the large ornaments. Since they had to decorate the tree on all sides, it took a lot of ornaments. But the lighting had to come first, and that would take Hunter and Mr Robinson at least a couple of hours.

It was lunchtime by the time Hunter and Ted had finished lighting the tree. Then they gave it a test run. Sally loved it when the tree lit up. Then the lights were shut off, and Mr Robinson shook hands with Hunter again, telling him it was good to work with him, just as he had always done with her father.

"Wow, I learned a lot today," Hunter said. He was rubbing his gloved hands together to get his fingers warm.

"I think we'd better go in and eat lunch and warm up first. Then we can come back and start decorating the tree."

"Will it really take us the rest of today and tomorrow to get it decorated?" Hunter asked as they walked toward the store.

"I'm afraid so. Hopefully we should finish early tomorrow afternoon."

"Okay. I'm going to go to the grocery store to buy me some lunch," Hunter said, starting in that direction.

"No. I brought you lunch today, too, to thank you for helping with the tree. It's in the fridge in the break room," Sally said, feeling a little embarrassed suddenly.

"Well, thanks, Sally. That was thoughtful of you." After a minute he added, "Of course, I shouldn't accept such a gesture. It might mean we're engaged."

Sally knew that he was making fun of her and she

couldn't blame him, but she thought she might play along a little bit. Coolly she said, "It's up to you, Hunter. It's risky, I know, but you don't have to tell anyone. Your lunch is in a separate sack with your name on it." She walked ahead of him, not looking back.

He ran after her and grabbed her arm, turning her around to face him. "You know I'm teasing you, don't you, Sally?"

"Yes, I do," she said firmly, "but I think it was lowdown of you to do so when I was only trying to be nice."

"That's all that I was trying to do the other night," Hunter said, again smiling mischievously at Sally.

"I know, but eating out is different. Everyone knows what you're doing. This is just a packed lunch."

"Okay, I'll accept your lunch, Sally, with gratitude." He looked at her, a stern look on his face, but his eyes were smiling.

Sally found herself smiling back as they walked into the store together, on good terms now. Hunter had been tempted to kiss her stubborn lips, but in the main street of Bailey, everyone would've seen. He didn't think Sally would like that.

He, on the other hand, would've liked kissing her anywhere. He'd found a real hunger for her kisses. He planned on walking her home again tonight and maybe kissing her again. It was all he had been able to think about, up there on that ladder. He had to kiss her again.

With that on his mind, when he found they were alone in the break room he seized the moment and grabbed her and kissed her.

"Hunter! What are you—"

A gasp from the door had both of them turning around to see Ethel standing there, her mouth open. "I—I—" and she turned and ran back into the store.

"Oh, great," Sally said. "That's just what we need."

"It doesn't matter, Sally, don't worry about it."

"Yes, it does matter, Hunter. Now, for sure, the entire town is going to be talking about us and are sure to think I'm heartbroken when you leave. They will all be feeling sorry for me!"

"I'll be feeling pretty sorry for *me* when I leave." Hunter stared at her as she removed two sacks from the refrigerator.

"Here's your lunch," she said shortly and sat down at the table.

"Aren't you going to say anything?"

"About what?"

"Me feeling sorry for myself when I leave. Don't you have anything to say?"

"Five minutes back in Denver and your time here will seem like a dream, Hunter. I know you have a busy life there."

"But I think I like it better here."

CHAPTER EIGHT

SALLY concentrated on her lunch, not looking at Hunter. She figured he was hoping to leave at least one broken heart when he headed back to Denver, and she didn't like the feeling that it would be hers.

"Sally, I'm being serious."

"Sure you are, Hunter. And I'm Santa Claus."

She still refused to meet his gaze. He finally opened his lunch sack and took out a sandwich. "Roast beef? Hey, that's great!"

Smiling slightly, to acknowledge his appreciation, she continued to eat. She'd included some cookies, but he hadn't found them yet. He got up to get both of them drinks, bringing a diet soda to her at the table.

"Thank you, Hunter."

"At least you're still talking to me."

"Of course I'm talking to you, Hunter. When you have something sensible to say."

"And you don't think my preferring life here in Bailey to that in Denver is sensible?"

"I think you like to think that, but I don't believe it's true."

"Why not? Don't you prefer life here to life in Denver?"

"Yes, but I've lived here all my life. Denver wouldn't suit me."

"So, if a guy came along and you fell in love with him and wanted to marry him, but you'd have to move to Denver, you'd say no, just because you don't want to leave Bailey?" He studied her as she composed her answer.

"I didn't say that, but I'd have to think long and hard about it. That would mean giving up the store, my heritage from my parents, and abandoning a way of life that I love. I'd be leaving Penny on her own, without any family around. It would be a hard decision."

"But you would consider it?" he asked curiously.

"I would consider it…but no, I don't think I'd choose that way of life."

"So what's so odd about me choosing this way of life?"

"You don't have any roots here. What would you do for a job? Work at my store?"

"Why not? I've done a good job, haven't I?"

"You've done a great job, Hunter, but I can't see you taking direction from me for the rest of your life."

"But I think you're the best boss I've ever worked for. You never make me feel small, or unimportant. You make me feel a part of the store's success. That's important."

"I hope so. I try to behave as Dad and Mom taught me. But it's very difficult doing all three of our jobs."

"That's why you need me."

"I need someone—someone who wants to be a part of my life. Not someone to work in the store."

They stared at each other and something passed between

them, but just then Susie came in to the back room, breaking the spell.

"Oh, hi, Hunter! I didn't know you were eating lunch now. Do you mind if I join you?"

Sally smiled ruefully and moved over so Susie could sit next to Hunter. For that, she received a dismissive smile.

"How do you like it here in Bailey, Hunter?" the girl asked, her eyes big as she stared at Hunter.

"I love it. Actually I don't want to go back to Denver," Hunter said, this time looking at Sally.

"Oh, no, you're kidding! Denver is so exciting! I'd love to go to Denver."

Since no conversation was required of Sally, she finished her sandwich quickly and left the table. She'd save her cookies until later. She went out into the store to see how Mary and Ethel were holding up. She sent Mary back to get her lunch and to supervise her child before Susie managed to force Hunter into a corner.

Ethel was delighted to welcome Sally to the floor and the two women chatted for a little while about the approaching Christmas Festival. Then Ethel moved away to greet a customer that had just entered the store.

Sally waited on an elderly gentleman and realized he was too embarrassed to ask for her help. She went to the break room door and asked Hunter if he could come help her for a moment. Hunter looked like she'd thrown a lifeline to him to escape a dangerous situation. She smiled, but simply said, "Mr Washington is shopping and could use your help."

The man looked as relieved as Hunter had only a

moment ago, and Sally moved on to the next customer. Susie emerged from the break room with red cheeks, as if her mother had given her a lecture, and began helping customers, too. Sally sent Ethel to have her lunch. As long as she and Hunter could take the time, it would be easier for the ladies to get their lunches eaten.

Twenty minutes later, Mary emerged and began helping customers. Sally signaled Hunter to join her when he finished with Mr Washington. A few minutes later, he appeared beside her. "Ready to go?"

"Yes, as long as you're thawed out."

"I am." They walked together out the front door and returned to the task of decorating the Christmas tree. Hunter decorated the top of the tree, and Sally worked on the middle branches. Hunter had less space to cover, but he had to move the ladder and come back down for each large ornament. Sally had to stretch up on her toes to hang the ornaments, but at least she didn't have to keep climbing up and down the ladder.

After several hours, they only had the bottom part of the tree to deal with. "I think we can finish before lunch tomorrow because you've been so efficient, Hunter."

"Really? That's great, Sally."

"Yes, you're really good at putting up decorations. You must've done it a lot at your grandfather's stores."

"Yeah. One year I was part of the maintenance crew who put up the decorations."

"Did you enjoy it?"

"Yeah. I even got to use my creativity, designing some of the decorations."

"When I was younger, I argued with Dad about always using the same old decorations. But he explained that buying new decorations would be difficult. That's why Mom and I decided to make our own."

Hunter laughed. "We've had a lot of the same experiences, haven't we?"

"Somewhat, but yours have been on a larger scale."

"That makes it less personal, Sally, I promise."

"I guess. Well, if you want to go home for the day, you've earned it, Hunter. You worked hard."

"I'd rather come back to the store with you."

"Why? Don't you want to put your feet up?"

"No, I'm fine. I'll come back with you. You might have another customer embarrassed to buy underwear from you."

"Is that what he wanted? How silly! But after he asked twice about a male salesperson, I didn't want to push him."

"Probably wise. He was greatly relieved when I appeared on the scene," Hunter said with a laugh.

"As you were when I called you away from Susie?"

"Damn, that girl has no shame. She keeps asking me if I want to sleep with her."

Sally stared at him. "What?"

"Yeah. She's afraid I'll get bored with no woman to sleep with while I'm in town, so she thought she'd volunteer."

"Her mother would be horrified!"

"Not according to Susie. She said she's quite experienced, sleeping with her boyfriend all the time. But she said he'd understand if she sleeps with me because, after all, I'm a Denver man."

"Oh, heavens, her mother would just die!"

"Are you sure she doesn't know?"

"I'm sure. I've heard her talk about how—how pure her daughter is. Such a good girl."

"Well, either she's a brazen liar, or her mother is mistaken."

"Oh, dear."

"Better compose yourself before we go in the store."

"Yes," Sally said, drawing a deep breath. Then she pasted on a smile. "How's this?"

"Perfect," he told her with a smile. Then he bent over and kissed her.

"Hunter!"

"I couldn't resist. You looked so cute."

"You're misbehaving as badly as Susie!"

"No! Surely not?"

"Go find some male customers to help."

"Yes, ma'am, boss lady," he teased as they entered the store.

Sally watched him walk across the store to the men's department and offer to help one of the customers. She couldn't hold back a smile at his teasing. His kisses were becoming quite addictive, too. All the more reason to avoid them.

Mary came rushing up to Sally. "Sally, I want you to know that I talked to Susie. She won't be chasing after Hunter anymore. I told her he was your man, and she should leave him alone."

Sally blinked several times. "Thank you, Mary, but that's not necessary. Hunter and I are friends, but he's going back to Denver on Christmas Eve." It seemed that the gossip was starting already and Sally steeled herself. It would only get worse when Hunter left.

"Maybe Hunter doesn't think that way," Mary said, smiling at Sally.

"I promise you, Mary, he does."

"Oh, well, keep your chin up, Sally. Maybe someone else just as nice will come along."

With a calm smile, Sally moved away, but inside she was muttering, "I'm going to kill Hunter Bedford!"

She went to the break room and got a soft drink to give herself time to compose herself. She hadn't expected anything from Hunter, but she hadn't asked to be consoled by the town, either.

Sitting there at the break table, drinking her cola, she tried to think of a way to appear undisturbed by Hunter's leaving. It would take a monumental acting job on her part. Because the truth was she was going to be heartbroken.

She sniffed, wishing she wasn't, but she didn't want to be alone again. Even more than that, she wanted a man who could share her life. Like Hunter.

"Don't be stupid," she muttered to herself.

"Who are you talking to?" Susie asked.

Sally heard the anger in her voice, but she wasn't going to say anything. "To myself. I've got some tough decisions to make about the store."

"Why? Are you thinking of selling up?"

"No, not at all. But I have to decide on some orders right away."

"Oh, that!" Susie said, dismissing Sally's concern as though it was nothing.

"I think my concern is real, Susie. After all, the store is my livelihood."

"Yeah, but other things are more important. Are you and Hunter serious about each other?"

"No, of course not!" Sally realized, too late, that Hunter would've preferred that she pretend to protect him from Susie's attention, but it was too late now.

"Oh. 'Cause Mom thought you were. She didn't want me to compete against you."

"I'm almost ten years older than you, Susie. I think I can manage on my own, without your mom's protection."

"Oh, yeah? Have you slept with him yet? That's how you get a guy, not by smiling at him."

Sally sighed and shook her head at the young girl's naïveté. "No, Susie, I haven't slept with him yet. Nor do I intend to. We're friends, that's all."

"Right," Susie said sarcastically.

"Are you already taking your break, Susie? I thought you just finished your lunch," Sally asked, suddenly angry at Susie's sheer cheek.

"I just wanted to get the lay of the land, so to speak. I'll go back to work now," she said with a smarmy smirk on her face.

Sally groaned and put her head in her hands. She knew that sleeping with Hunter wouldn't guarantee he stayed. But Sally wished she could think of another way of talking him into staying. After he went back to Denver, she'd have her life in ruins.

Taking a deep breath, she got up and went back into the store to help with the many shoppers.

* * *

Hunter started clearing the dressing rooms in the men's department at a quarter until eight. He was tired and ready to call it a night. He felt sure Sally felt the same. And she didn't even have to put up with Susie's pursuit. He wasn't sure why the girl was flirting with him again, but she'd been going nonstop since they'd come in from working on the tree.

There were still a number of shoppers in the store. But he was relieved when Sally told Mary and Susie they could collect their belongings and go home. As soon as Ethel finished with her customer, Sally released her, also.

Susie came out of the break room and crossed over to the men's department. Hunter almost groaned as the girl approached him.

"Hunter, want to come over?" she asked with a wink.

"No, thanks, Susie. I'm pretty tired tonight."

"Time is running out, Hunter. You won't be here much longer."

"True. But not tonight, Susie."

"Fine! I offered!"

"Yes, you certainly did," he said and gave her a direct look, figuring she couldn't mistake his rejection.

She stuck her nose in the air and turned to walk to the front door where her mother was waiting for her.

Hunter looked for Sally and noticed she had a customer who was still shopping. He went to the counter and took out some boxes, so he could help Sally with the purchases the woman was making.

Sally brought the woman to the cash register and while ringing her up, Sally began directing Hunter about the boxing of the gifts. "Did you want us to gift-wrap these purchases?" Hunter asked the lady.

"No, I'll wrap them when I get home, but I do appreciate the boxes."

"We're glad to provide them. Thanks, Hunter," Sally said, smiling at him.

The woman looked at Hunter also. "I think it's nice you are helping Sally out in the store, young man. This season has been a little difficult for her."

"I think she's doing a fine job, ma'am," Hunter said solemnly.

"Well, yes, of course! But, you know, it's just been hard."

"Yes, ma'am, I do," Hunter assured her with a smile.

"Well, thanks for staying open late, Sally. I'm glad to get all my shopping done."

"It's all right, Carol." Sally followed the lady and unlocked the door and held it open. "Good night."

When she locked the front door and pulled down the shades, she smiled wearily at Hunter. "Did Susie come after you again?"

"Yeah. Do you know why?"

"I think that might be my fault. When she asked me if we were serious, I answered without thinking. I told her no."

"Damn it, Sally, couldn't you have said something else? Now I'll never get rid of her."

"I'm sorry, Hunter, but I'm not going to lie to protect you!"

Hunter looked at Sally, serious for a moment. "Are you sure it would be a lie, Sally?"

"Don't start that silliness again, Hunter. You know it

would. You don't intend to stay here. And I don't want to deal with everyone's sadness for me when you leave."

"Yeah," he seemingly agreed, looking around the store. "Okay, let's go home," he said, as if they were going to the same home.

Sally paused for a moment at his words. Home. With Hunter. The idea made her insides tingle as she thought about what that might be like. What would it be like to close the store every night and walk the short distance home holding Hunter's hand? They would make dinner together and then sit at the table, discussing the day's events. But that was never going to happen, because Hunter was leaving for Denver and Sally would be alone again. She sighed and met Hunter's gaze. "Certainly, it's been a long day."

"You wouldn't consider fixing me a sandwich, would you?" Hunter asked.

Sally paused. Then she looked at him again. "Of course, I can do that. You've worked hard today." It couldn't hurt to extend their evening just a little longer and Sally smiled in return and led the way to the back door, stopping to collect her coat and purse and keys. Hunter grabbed his coat and followed her.

Outside, he waited until she'd locked the door. Then he walked across the street with her to her home. He was beginning to love the home as well as the lady. He couldn't believe he was thinking about not going back to Denver. But life in Bailey fit him like a glove, as much as Sally fit him.

Inside the house, Sally turned on lights as they moved through to the kitchen.

"This room has such nice smells," he announced.

Sally smiled at him. "Yes, it does. I think it's all the baking I've been doing lately."

"Like my grandmother's kitchen. After she died, almost no one used the kitchen and the smell eventually faded away, just like her memory."

"That must have been difficult, but you still remember her."

"Yeah. But I remember her more when I'm here."

"That's nice, Hunter. I'm glad my home makes you feel so comfortable." She turned to the fridge and took several dishes out and set them on the counter. "I think instead of a sandwich we'll finish off the roast beef with some veggies. Is that okay?"

"It sounds great," he said with enthusiasm.

"It had better be to make up for turning Susie down."

"That wasn't even a strain. She doesn't interest me."

"She is cute, you know," Sally teased.

"Yeah, for a teenager, I guess so. I'm more interested in older ladies," he said, giving her a sexy look.

"Oh. Shall I warn Mrs Grabowski that you've got your eye on her?"

"Not quite that old. I'm thinking somewhere around twenty-five, close to twenty-six."

"Nice try, but I'm not falling for any of that big city talk."

"Damn, where did I go wrong?"

She laughed, hoping it hid her heartache. "You underestimated your audience." She put the roast beef in the microwave and took out a skillet and filled it with mixed vegetables.

"Shall I set the table?" he asked.

"Yes, please. Napkins are in the pantry."

It didn't take him long to set two places. Then he got out two glasses and filled them with ice. Taking the pitcher out of the refrigerator, he poured the two glasses full and set them on the table.

"Anything else I can do?"

"No, that's all. This will be ready in a few minutes."

He introduced several topics related to the store and they talked business until the meal was ready.

When she joined him at the table, she took a big sip of her iced tea. "Oh, that tastes good."

"Yeah. I like the way you keep a pitcher in the fridge, always ready."

"Mom did that when I became a teen. She'd encourage me to drink tea rather than always drinking colas."

"Smart lady."

"Yeah, she and her brother were quite bright. Dad was, too, but he always teased Mom that he chose her for her brains."

"I find that hard to believe if she looked anything like you," he said with a smile.

"Another example of your city slicker ways!" she exclaimed. "I know you've seen the pictures of my mom in the den."

"That I have. Like you, she was a beauty. Do you and your cousin look alike?"

"Not really. Penny is a little taller than me and she has dark hair."

"Really? I would've thought you looked alike."

"No. We think a lot alike, though."

"So she's resistant to city slicker talk, too?"

"I don't know. Right now, I think she's listening to a ranch manager who's mighty good-looking."

"You like him?" Hunter asked, suddenly looking grim.

"Me? No, of course not!"

"Good." He smiled and took a bite of roast beef. "This meat is really good, and tender, too."

After dinner, he insisted on helping clean up.

"You're certainly easy to work with, Hunter."

"Thank you, ma'am. I think I could say the same thing about you. Well, I think I better be making a move, it's getting late."

She smiled and as he gathered his belongings Sally escorted him to the door to send him on his way.

At the door, he suddenly turned and took her by her shoulders. Then he bent and kissed her good night.

Sally knew she should protest and pushing slightly on his wide chest she said his name, "Hunter—"

That was all she managed before he kissed her again, a deep, soul-touching kiss this time and Sally knew that if she didn't draw away now, she'd never be able to.

"Hunter. I—I have to—to go to bed, now."

"Alone?" he whispered.

"Yes! Yes, alone. I'll see you tomorrow."

"Okay. Tomorrow." Then he kissed her again, before he walked through her front door, closing it behind him.

Then she heard him walk away.

CHAPTER NINE

FRIDAY morning, they finished decorating the tree.

"Hey, you know, this tree looks pretty good," Hunter said as he stood in front of it.

"Yes, it does, doesn't it? Of course, the tree itself is magnificent."

"Yeah. Penny did a good job picking it out."

"Yes, she did," Sally said with a sigh.

"What's wrong?" Hunter hurriedly asked, taking a step closer to Sally.

"Nothing! But—but I was concerned that we couldn't pull off all the Christmas stuff that our parents managed every year. And it looks like we will. It's a relief, if things go well tomorrow night."

Hunter put his arm around her and leaned over to kiss her forehead. "I think you and Penny have been superb. You've managed to run the store by yourself, with satisfied customers, as far as I can tell, and pulled together the town Festival. What more could you do?"

"Probably a lot. I haven't even put up a tree at the house, but I'm so seldom there," she admitted with another sigh.

"It would look nice in the living room, near the fireplace."

She turned to stare at him. "That's where we always put it. Then, when we got home, Dad would turn on the lights. It made the room look magical."

"There's still time. Christmas isn't until Thursday."

"No, I don't think I have the energy. Besides, decorating a tree by myself doesn't seem—I'm being silly. Let's go have lunch," she said, stepping away from his arm.

"Sure, that's a good idea. I'm really hungry today."

"I brought your lunch again today. It isn't roast beef, but I hope you'll like it."

"Now I can truly say I always like your cooking, Sally," he said with a big grin.

She smiled at him and led the way to the store. When they entered, the store was exceptionally busy. "Let's go take off our coats and see if we can help out a little before we eat."

"Okay," he agreed, not complaining about the delay of lunch.

It was almost an hour before Sally sent Susie and Mary to eat their lunch. Technically they should've received a half hour lunch, but Mary came back to work after fifteen minutes.

"Thank you, Mary," Sally said with a smile. "I'll try to give you a break when things slow down."

"I'm fine." Mary started helping customers.

Sally suggested Hunter and Ethel go to lunch next. Ethel headed for the break room at once. Hunter, however, said he would wait for her.

"Hunter, you really should go now. Susie is almost due back on the floor, and Ethel is in the break room, which should restrain Susie's conversation a little."

"No, I'll wait for you."

"I thought I was the one who was hardheaded?" she demanded in exasperation.

"I learned from the very best," he said with a grin and turned back to help another customer.

Sally, too, returned to helping customers, but she had a smile on her face, put there by Hunter's response.

Finally, when all three women had returned to work, Sally waved to Hunter and headed for the break room. He finished with his customer and followed Sally.

"You're doing incredible business today," he said with a sigh as he sat down.

"I know. I don't think it's ever been this busy. I thought tomorrow would be our busiest day."

"It may yet be, but we've finished the Christmas tree. At least we have that out of the way."

"True, but the store will be busy when you're playing Santa Claus, too."

"You are coming out with me, aren't you?"

"I guess so. It doesn't seem fair to throw you to the wolves all alone."

Hunter looked at her from under his brows. "I should think not!"

"I'll call Penny tonight. She can be Jake's assistant and I'll be yours."

"Good. That will make everything easier."

She took out her sandwich and started to eat, afraid she wouldn't get her full half hour. Hunter, too, began eating, with sporadic conversation.

Sally had only been there ten minutes when Susie

entered the break room saying she had a problem and needed her to come help.

"I'll wrap up what's left and put it in the fridge before I come out," Hunter told her.

Sally got up and left the room. By the time she'd satisfied the shopper, who had been offended by Susie's attitude, there were lines forming in front of her for service. She was tempted to call Hunter to help her, but she was becoming too dependent on the man. And he'd be leaving after Christmas.

She tried to erase that thought, but it lingered in her mind. When Hunter suddenly appeared and took some of those waiting in line, she smiled at him, but she kept reminding herself she'd have to learn to manage on her own.

Neither of them got to eat supper that evening, until she'd locked the front door on the last customer. Mary, Susie and Ethel had left at eight o'clock, but they had a couple of late shoppers and she and Hunter had stayed to serve them.

"Thanks for staying so late, Hunter," Sally said as she turned away from the locked front door.

"You know I'm not going to leave you alone."

"I know, but there won't be anyone to stay with me after you leave. I should get used to handling things on my own."

"Hmm. That may be true, but until I'm gone, I'll stay with you and see you home. I want to be sure you're safe."

"I know," she said softly, thinking how nice that sounded. She'd never thought she would lean on someone as she was with Hunter. She hoped he didn't mind.

When they crossed to her house, she hesitantly invited

him in for a late supper. It was becoming something of a tradition between the two of them. To her surprise, he shook his head.

"But where are you going to get some supper?"

"The Diamond Back is still open. I can drop by there and get some dinner. Go on in and get some rest." Then he bent and kissed her lips. "Now go."

She went into the house alone and locked the door. Then she heard him call, "Good night."

It seemed senseless to fix a real meal for just herself. Instead she made a little bowl of oatmeal for her dinner. After her uninspired meal, she curled up on the sofa in front of the fire in the living room. Slowly she looked around the room and imagined how it had felt only a couple of nights ago when she and Hunter had sat drinking coffee. They had talked about business and their family and Sally thought she had never felt so content. If only Hunter was staying for a little while longer, who knows what might have happened between them.

Finally she gave up. Why bother? He was going to be gone by Christmas. Had she fallen for him simply because she was feeling alone? After considering that idea, she rejected it. No, she'd fallen for him because—because he fit her like a glove. He understood her work, and he'd made such a thing of "keeping her safe." She knew she was safe here in Bailey, but with Hunter around she felt even more so, more than she had ever done before.

Laying her head on the back of the sofa and staring into the fire, she decided she couldn't explain her feelings. How she wished her parents were with her so that she could talk to them about her feelings. Maybe she could talk to Penny about Hunter…on Christmas Day. They were supposed to have Christmas dinner then, here in town. Just the two of them.

Sally shed a few more tears for her parents. Then she wiped away her tears and went to bed. She was so very tired tonight.

Saturday morning, people were lined up outside the store waiting for them to open so Sally and Hunter had their hands full.

Sally took a minute to call both Mary and Ethel and told them any help they could give her would be greatly appreciated.

Ethel arrived fifteen minutes later. Mary and Susie got there by ten o'clock.

All the customers praised Sally for getting the tree decorated. She told all of them she couldn't have done it without Hunter's assistance.

There was a festive air in the store that day. Sally knew they were doing an incredible business. Which only made her miss her parents more. But at least she hadn't let them down. She'd managed to pull off everything.

As the time grew closer to the beginning of the Christmas Festival, the store grew even more crowded. She managed to give each of the ladies assisting her an hour's rest, because they would be on their own from six-thirty to eight. And Sally was staying open an extra hour this evening.

She'd dug out her father's Santa suit and the disguise

makeup, preparing it for Hunter. She couldn't help smiling, thinking about her father in the Santa suit. She'd been six when she finally figured out who played Santa. She first figured out that her uncle was the early Santa. So she'd switched to the later Santa, and found out it was her dad.

Tonight, there would be two new Santas.

But at least they were having Santas. Her mother and father would be proud of her, she knew. And Penny, too. Together, they'd managed to continue on, as she knew her parents, and Penny's, too, had expected them to do.

At four-thirty, Penny and her ranch manager, Jake, arrived at the store, ready to change him into Santa. Sally slipped back to the break room to help them. "Are you ready to be Santa, Jake?" she asked.

"I guess. I'm a little worried about it."

"Don't be. You'll have Penny with you."

After she sent them out to the town circle, which had tables set up around it to offer used goods and the refreshments they provided, she returned to the front of the store.

"Hunter, if you want some time at the Festival before your start as Santa, you can go," she whispered to him.

"I'll go out when they turn on the tree lights," he whispered back before he helped another customer.

Sally wanted to go out then, too. But when Hunter slipped out, the store was still crowded. She didn't feel she could leave the store.

Hunter came in a few minutes later. "The tree looks great, Sally."

"Good. You need to get in the Santa suit. I'll come help in just a minute."

When she got to the break room, he had the Santa suit on, the pillows properly stuffed into place. She smiled. The costume certainly changed Hunter's appearance. "Ready for your beard and eyebrows?"

"Yeah. Do your worst," he said, sitting down so she could attach the white hair.

With great care, she used glue from her makeup kit and started with the eyebrows. Then she added the beard. Suddenly Hunter had completely disappeared, transformed into dear old Santa. She added the Santa hat with white hair attached.

"Okay, you're done," Sally said, offering a mirror to Hunter.

"Is that me?"

"It had better be."

Just then the door opened and they found themselves facing a second Santa Claus.

Sally introduced Hunter to Penny and Jake. Then, with a Santa hat on her head and a red sweater on, she led Hunter out to the big seat by the tree that Jake had abandoned.

"Some of these kids look a little older," Hunter whispered as he sat down in the chair.

"Yes, the younger ones are usually the first to come because of their early bedtimes. Then the slightly older ones come, even if they don't believe in Santa anymore."

Sally motioned for the first child to step up to Santa's chair, and they began.

When they had finally ended, Hunter had handled his role perfectly, but he was ready for it to be over. Sally pushed Hunter back toward the store. "Okay, Santa, you go and get changed now and then I've got to get back and see how everyone is doing," she reminded Hunter.

They got in the store but before Hunter could discard his costume, Susie threw her arms around his neck.

"Santa! Don't you want to know what I want for Christmas?"

Hunter tried to dislodge Susie's arms, but she whispered in his ear something that disconcerted him. His eyes widened, but he renewed his efforts to get her to turn loose. Sally knew the person to help him. She signaled for Mary.

Mary immediately called her daughter to order. "Susie, turn loose of him at once!"

After planting a big kiss on Santa, Susie released him and whirled away to wait on customers.

Hunter reached the back room, with Sally following.

"Are you all right?"

"I'm just glad she didn't climb into my lap out there."

"What did she whisper in your ear?" Sally asked curiously.

"More of the same stuff she's been offering all along, only a little more—more personal this time."

Sally rolled her eyes. "Come on. I'll take off your fur."

He sat down and let her take off the eyebrows and then the beard. He moaned in ecstasy as he scratched his cheeks and chin. "Ah, that feels so good."

"I know. Dad used to complain about the makeup itching, too," Sally said, smiling in sympathy. "I've got to get back out on the floor. After you change, feel free to go home or go get some supper. You don't need to work the rest of the evening."

She hurried back into the store without hearing an actual

answer from Hunter. She had too much to deal with to concern herself with his decision.

When she turned around a few minutes later to discover Hunter helping a customer, she couldn't hold back a smile. He'd done as he'd always done. Been there for her.

When nine o'clock came, Sally locked the front door so no one could come in and rushed the last few shoppers out the door.

"Thanks to all of you for your hard work today," she said with a weary smile.

Mary, Susie and Ethel slipped out right away.

Hunter grabbed her arm. "We'll clean up tomorrow. We've got dinner ordered at the Diamond Back. It's supposed to be on the table by nine-fifteen. They're open until ten tonight. So we need to hurry over there or our food will get cold."

"But—but I could—"

"Nope. We're off to the restaurant."

Their brisk walk to the Diamond Back was actually invigorating. Sally didn't have anything to fix for dinner anyway. She was looking forward to a good meal. And she was looking forward to spending the evening with Hunter.

Inside the restaurant, there were other diners. But on their table, dinner was already set out.

Sally laughed when she saw the enchiladas on her plate.

"How perfect! Thank you, Hunter."

"I just wanted to be sure you had a good dinner. What did you eat last night?"

"Oatmeal. I was too tired to make much else."

"Well, eat your dinner. I ordered dessert, also."

"You did? I'm not sure—"

"Too late. It's already ordered. Their coconut cream pie."

"Oh, dear. Now I'll have to go on a diet."

When they'd finished their meal, Hunter paid for the dinner, refusing any argument by Sally. Then, with their coats and gloves on, he took her hand and walked her back to her house.

"That was a delightful meal, Hunter. I was too tired to cook, so it was perfect. I had a really good time tonight," Sally said, looking fondly at Hunter and enjoying the feeling of him holding her hand.

"I'm glad. Now, I think I should tell you that when we get to your house I'm going to kiss you good night. I'm not coming in and I'm not going to kiss you more than once. That's too dangerous. Okay?"

Sally was silent for a moment before she answered, taking in Hunter's words. "Okay." It was definitely too dangerous for him to kiss her more than once. With the knowledge that their time together was limited to one kiss outside her house, she slid her arms around his neck and reciprocated his kiss.

"Man, I wish I hadn't promised all those things," he said with a sigh after he'd kissed her. "Okay, go in and lock your door. I'll see you tomorrow."

She did as he told her to do, leaning against the door once she'd locked it, knowing he was walking back to the bed-and-breakfast. Alone.

Suddenly she realized he'd said he'd see her tomorrow. She hadn't planned on going in to the store tomorrow, but maybe she could change her plans. For Hunter.

* * *

Sally didn't set the alarm the next morning. She was going to sleep until she woke, and she didn't care if that meant sleeping until noon.

When the phone rang, waking her up, the first thing she did was look at her watch. It was eight o'clock! It could only be one person calling at this time—Hunter. She couldn't believe he'd call so early.

And that's exactly what she said when she answered the phone.

The silence her comment made alerted her to a mistake. "I'm sorry. I thought this was—I beg your pardon. Who is this, please?"

"Good morning, Miss Rogers. It's Wilbur Hunt, here. Where's my grandson?"

Sally sat upright in her bed. "Good morning, Mr Hunt. Erm, I assume he's at the bed-and-breakfast where he's staying. Have you tried calling that number?"

"Bed-and-breakfast? No! This is the only number he gave me."

"Just one moment, let me get the number for you." Sally got out of bed and found the small phone book for the Bailey area. Then she picked up the receiver again. "Mr Hunt, the number is 555-4703."

"Thank you. I'm planning on my grandson coming home today, Miss Rogers. That won't be a problem for you, will it?"

Sally recognized the answer he was wanting. She'd known it would come. But she didn't want Hunter to go. "No, Mr Hunt, that won't be a problem at all. If that's what Hunter wants to do."

"Of course it's what he wants. Boy's been gone too long already! I need him here."

"Yes, I'm sure you do."

"I'll call him."

"Okay. Goodbye, Mr Hunt."

Sally fell back among her pillows, trying to stem the tears that filled her eyes. She'd known Hunter would be leaving, so why was she being so silly? Because she'd wanted him to stay so badly.

She sniffed several times and gradually closed her eyes again. Yesterday had taken a lot of energy. She needed more sleep.

When she woke up again, it was almost eleven. Her first thought was that Hunter would be already gone. He hadn't even called to say goodbye.

She climbed out of bed, still feeling tired. It was almost tempting not to get dressed, but she knew she'd be embarrassed if anyone stopped by and found her in her nightgown.

She dressed and went down to the kitchen to start a pot of coffee. While it was perking, she mixed up hot cakes. They seemed to fit her mood. Just as the griddle heated up, the doorbell rang.

Setting aside the bowl of batter and turning off the fire under the griddle, she hurried to the front door, swinging it open.

Hunter stood there, a smile on his face.

Sally drew up, trying to keep the tears at bay. "Hello. Did you stop by to say goodbye? You didn't need to do that."

He frowned. "Goodbye? What are you talking about?"

"Didn't your grandfather call you?"

"Sure. But how did you know?"

"You gave him my number."

"Yeah, for emergencies. I also gave him the number at the bed-and-breakfast. Did he call you here?"

"Yes, at eight o'clock this morning."

"I'm sorry about that, Sally, I had no idea. Aren't you going to ask me in?"

Sally drew a deep breath and then stepped back. She could let him come in for a few minutes to tell her goodbye. Why should she freeze to death standing in the open door?

"Mmm, I smell coffee," Hunter said rubbing his hands together.

"Yes, would you like a cup?"

"Yeah, that would be great." He followed her into the kitchen.

She poured him a cup of coffee and then stood there, waiting for him to announce his departure.

Instead he said, "Mind if I sit down?"

"Of course not."

"Aren't you going to have coffee?"

"Why don't we just get this over with, Hunter?" she asked.

"Get what over with? Do you have someplace to go?"

"No, but I believe you do."

"Not me." He took a sip of his coffee.

"Your grandfather told me he wanted you to go home, so stop pretending! You're here to say goodbye so let's just get it over with."

CHAPTER TEN

HUNTER was silent for a long time and frowned at Sally. "Do you think I'm a child, Sally? Jumping to obey when someone tells me to do something?"

Sally drew back. "Are you telling me that your grandfather is lying? He said he needed you."

Hunter grinned. "Of course he needs me. He's a control freak. He wants to know where everyone is at any minute. He can't be sure what I'm doing here exactly, so he wants me back in town."

"But he sounded very urgent. I expected you to stay until Christmas Eve, but if you want to go now, I can spare you."

"Mmm, actually, I think I'd rather stay here. What's in that bowl?" Hunter asked, pointing at the mixing bowl on the table.

"Pancake batter, you're welcome to stay. But what about your grandfather. Surely he is all alone?" she pointed out.

"My grandfather has a housekeeper and an assistant who jumps any time he wants something. I think I'd like some pancakes."

Sally, still distracted by what Hunter was saying, automatically turned on the burners under the griddle. "Where's your mother?"

"I believe she's skiing in Switzerland."

Sally turned to stare at him. "Skiing?"

"Yeah, she likes the après-ski life."

"Will she come back for Christmas?"

Hunter shrugged his shoulders. "Doesn't matter. If she does, she and Granddad will argue nonstop. It's not very pleasant. Is the griddle hot enough now?"

"Yes," she said absentmindedly, scooping up the batter to put it on the grill. "Why do they argue?"

"Because she won't do what he wants her to do."

"What is that?"

"Take an interest in the business. He wants to make her president of his company, keep it in the family, but he doesn't think she knows enough about the business. He's right, of course."

Sally turned the pancakes, golden-brown on one side. "But you're learning the business. Isn't that enough?"

"No. It's not enough for Granddad. He feels Mother should be a good mother to me, and a good daughter to him, and nothing else."

"What do you think?" she asked, frowning as she scooped up the finished pancakes and set them in front of him.

"I think I need some butter and syrup."

"What?" she asked, startled by his request. Then she nodded. "Yes, of course."

When she set those on the table, she turned to make her own pancakes. While they were cooking, she poured herself a cup of coffee. Then she took up her pancakes and joined him at the table.

"What I think is that she has the right to live her own life. But my mother is used to having the money she wants. She never turns down Granddad's money, but she won't work for it. That drives him crazy."

"Aren't you working for him?"

"I was."

Her fork was halfway to her mouth when she realized what he'd said. She lowered the bite of pancakes back to her plate. "What are you saying, Hunter?"

"When I went back to Denver that first night, I told him I thought I'd found a place I wanted to be, at least for a while. And I gave him my resignation."

"You resigned? But that means there was no reason for you to work at the store. You wouldn't even let me pay you! I wouldn't have accepted your help if I'd known you were doing it for free! That's crazy!"

"No, I think it's the sanest thing I've ever done. Now, I have an important question to ask you."

Sally stared at him, wondering what could come out of his mouth next. "Yes?"

"Can you ice skate?"

Her eyes grew even wider and she continued to stare at him.

"Well?"

With a frown, she said, "Yes, I can ice skate."

"Good. Finish your breakfast and we'll go ice skating."

After a moment of thinking, Sally smiled. She wasn't going to win this battle with Hunter so she might as well enjoy his company whilst she still could. "All right, Hunter. I haven't ice skated this winter. There was always too much going on. Ice skating sounds like a good idea."

"I asked the lady who runs the bed-and-breakfast. She told me her kids were going skating this afternoon. When I asked her where they skated, she told me about a pond nearby that the locals used."

"Yes, the Browns' pond. They have always invited the town to join them."

"Good. I'm glad you know the place, because I didn't understand the directions she gave me." He took another bite of the pancakes. "These are really good, by the way."

"Thank you."

Suddenly her heart felt decidedly light. "You do know how to ice skate, too, don't you, Hunter?"

"Yeah, but it's been a while. You may have to hold me up for a little while."

She chuckled. "It might be good to see you do something less than expertly. I haven't, yet."

"Aw, shucks, lady, you flatter me."

"No, I don't."

"How about another round of pancakes?"

"You're still hungry?"

"I'm a growing boy."

With a shake of her head, she returned to the stove and put on two more pancakes. When they were done, she set them in front of Hunter. "Now, I'm going up to get dressed for an ice skating trip. I'll be down in a minute."

Hunter watched her go, glad to see excitement in her walk. He'd been worried about her last night. She'd been so very tired. If he'd known his grandfather had called her because he'd thought his grandson was sleeping with her, he'd have been a lot ruder to him this morning.

He was tempted to pick up the phone and call his grandfather at once. But he wasn't going to do that. He was going to take Sally ice skating because she needed to do something fun and unrelated to business. That was more important than chewing out the old man today.

Especially since he had a shock coming for him in a few days, if things went well.

He heard Sally coming down the stairs as he rinsed the dishes and put them in the dishwasher. He'd already put away the butter and syrup.

She walked into the kitchen and looked around her in surprise. "You cleaned the kitchen?"

"Only fair, since I ate breakfast here."

"I like the way you think!"

"Thank you, ma'am. Ready to go skating?"

"Yes, I am."

A few minutes later, they parked close to the pond where a number of people were skating. A barrel beside the pond had a fire going in it so the skaters could warm up every round or two.

Hunter got their skates and Sally jumped out of the car, eager to get started. There was a bench near the fire for putting on their skates and a wooden shelf to store their shoes while they were skating.

Sally watched how quickly Hunter laced up his skates. "You do that awfully well. Are you sure you can't skate much?"

"I didn't say I couldn't skate. I just said I was a little rusty. I haven't skated since college, I guess. And that's been about eight years."

"Okay," Sally said slowly. "Are you ready?"

"Sure." He reached out for her hand.

Sally let him take her hand, clad in wool gloves, and he led her to the edge of the pond. They stepped out on the ice and began to glide. He reached for her other hand and they skated along, their arms linked.

"You faker! You can skate well!"

"Nothing fancy, just straight skating."

"And here I thought you'd be falling all over me, pulling me down. You skate much better than me."

"No, I don't. And it won't be long before you have to hold me up. I'll tire easily."

"Sore ankles?"

"Yeah. Hey, let's skate over here," he suggested, following the curve of the pond.

They almost bumped into another couple. Sally introduced Hunter to Chris and Linda Barton. She'd gone to high school with both of them. Chris and Linda had gone steady in high school, but then Chris had gone away to school and they'd broken up. When Chris had returned to the family ranch after college, they'd reconnected and married almost at once. Sally was delighted to see them both now.

Skating as a foursome so they could chat while they skated, they made several rounds of the pond before they stopped at the barrel to warm up.

Hunter and Chris were deep in conversation when Linda

whispered something to Sally, who immediately congratu-
lated her friend. Hunter noticed what was going on, but he
said nothing.

Later when the two of them were skating alone again,
he asked Sally what Linda had told her.

"She told me she's pregnant! They'd been wanting a
child for several years. I'm very pleased for them," Sally
said, smiling.

"That's great. Good for them. I liked Chris a lot. He
seems like a great guy."

"He is. He's managing his dad's ranch right now, since
he had a heart attack last year."

"That must put a lot of stress on Chris."

"Maybe, but he wanted to run the operation. His sister
has no interest in it, though she wants the money from it,
kind of like your mother I suppose."

"Ah. Well, that happens. But I'm glad Chris is happy
with everything."

"Yes, he and Linda have their own house on the ranch."

"That will make having a baby easier."

"I guess, if it's ever easier."

"It's easy for a man to say that, honey. They don't ever
get pregnant."

She gave him an exasperated look. "I did know that,
Hunter!"

"I kind of figured you did," he confessed with a grin.
Then he circled her and made her spin. When she came out
of the spin, she found herself in his arms.

"That was not straight skating!"

"I'm remembering a little more."

For an hour they skated around the pond, meeting and talking to people. While Sally elected to warm by the barrel, he ran races with some of the teenage boys. Sally laughed, watching him act like a teenager himself.

She couldn't remember the last time she'd had such a relaxing time. Definitely not since her parents died. And she hadn't expected it. But she'd desperately needed it. How had Hunter known?

When he led her out for another couple of rounds of the pond, she said, "Hunter, I didn't realize I needed to relax so badly, but I want to thank you. This has been a wonderful afternoon."

"I'm glad you enjoyed it. It seemed to me all you've done since I met you is work. Work is admirable, but you know the old saying, all work and no play, et cetera."

"Yes, I know. I just—I was trying so hard to meet my parents' expectations. I probably couldn't have taken a day like today until after the Festival. But today is perfect. Now I think I can make it until Christmas."

"I hope so." And he leaned down and kissed her.

"Hunter! People can see us!"

"You think they'll be shocked that their favorite store owner is being kissed?"

"No, but I told you I don't want people thinking that I'll be heartbroken when you're gone and them feeling sorry for me."

"Mmm, I guess that's smart thinking on your part…"

"Yes, I suppose it is," she said sadly.

"So it's okay if I kiss you as long as I'm here, right?"

"No! That's not what I meant!"

He laughed down at her. "Oh, I get it. I can kiss you as much as I like as long as we're in private."

She couldn't help responding to his teasing. "Well, that's closer to what I meant."

"Good," he whispered in her ear, his arm wrapped around her as he skated her around the pond.

After several more rounds, they returned to the bench and took off their skates and replaced them with their shoes. "Walking seems strange now, doesn't it?" he asked.

"Yes," she agreed and then stumbled.

His arm shot around her again. "Steady there."

"Sorry, I didn't mean—"

"Don't pull away. We'll make better progress if we stick together. Besides, it's warmer that way."

When they got in Hunter's car, they sat waiting while his engine warmed up. He leaned toward her and said, "You know what would really be perfect now?"

"A cup of hot chocolate?"

"That and a big hot pizza. I don't suppose Bailey has a pizzaria?"

"Yes, we do, it's a lovely place, but they don't deliver."

"Do they do takeout?"

"Yes, but we can eat it there. They have a big open fireplace and the tables are all placed around the fire. It's lovely there."

"Why haven't you told me about this place before now?"

Sally blinked several times. Then she confessed, "I didn't think you'd eat at such a—a lowly place. I mean, there are no tablecloths or fancy menus, just a blackboard list of the kinds of pizzas they make."

"Ah, Sally, you don't really know me, do you? I don't have to have a tablecloth or a fancy menu. A good pizza is worth a lot more. Tell me how to get to this place."

Sally gave him directions and they arrived at the pizzaria on one of the few back streets in Bailey.

There were four or five couples sprinkled around the big fireplace. Hunter and Sally chose one of the empty tables and a young waitress arrived at their table almost at once.

"What do you like on your pizza, Sally?" Hunter asked.

"Almost anything but anchovies."

"Perfect," he murmured and ordered a pizza with about five toppings on it. "And we want the biggest size. We're starving!"

"Hunter," she whispered, as the girl left the table. "We'll never be able to finish a big one."

"So we'll have leftovers for tomorrow evening. That won't be so bad, will it?"

"That might be absolutely wonderful. But we're closing at seven tomorrow and Tuesday. And then, on Wednesday, we'll close at four. Of course, you'll probably want to leave at noon so you get back to Denver before it gets dark."

"We'll see."

"I don't think we'll be too busy. I think everyone has bought everything they'll need by now. We'll get a few last minute shoppers or people who have forgotten something, but the big rush is over."

"What will you do with yourself with all that time on your hands?" he asked with a smile.

"Well, I need to do some baking. I may make cookies tonight. And Wednesday evening, I'll bake a cake and several pies for our Christmas dinner. I think I told you Penny was coming to my house for Christmas dinner."

"That's right. Has she called and asked if Jake can come?"

Sally sat up straight. "What? Why would you ask that?"

"They seemed awfully close at the Christmas Festival, and I saw him kiss her before they left the store to go play Santa."

"No! Did you really?"

"I did. And she didn't protest very much, either."

"She didn't say anything to me about it!"

"Maybe she was afraid it would make you feel too much alone, if she told you," Hunter said softly.

"Yes, I suppose so," Sally replied, suddenly thoughtful.

"I have an idea," Hunter said, breaking the somber mood. "Why don't you invite me to Christmas dinner, too?"

"Invite you to—why would I do that?"

"So Penny and Jake won't feel awkward."

"Hunter, of course you're welcome to Christmas dinner, but I suspect your grandfather wants you at his house for Christmas."

"Oh, there'll be plenty of time for that. He doesn't usually have his Christmas dinner till later at night. I'd still have time to get there if I left by three."

"Really? Then yes, I'd love to have you stay for Christmas dinner with me and Penny…and Jake if you really think he'll come, too."

"He'll come."

"I'll just take your word for it, will I?"

"Only if you're smart," he teased.

The waitress brought out their drinks and the large pizza.

"Whoa! I didn't know your big pizzas were quite so large," he said with a smile at the girl.

"Yes, sir. Here are your plates. Can I get you anything else?"

"No, thanks. But it looks really good."

She walked away with a smile.

"Well, how about it? How many pieces do you want to start with?"

"How about one? One at a time works best."

"I guess. In high school, when I shared a pizza, I learned to grab more than one, or I wouldn't get a second piece."

"I promise I don't eat it that fast!"

"Okay, one at a time."

They ate for a while in silence, both enjoying the hot, tasty pizza. Sally thought again how easy it was to sit with Hunter and share a meal. She was going to miss him terribly when he'd gone. As if he could read her thoughts Hunter interrupted the silence.

"I really enjoyed the Christmas Festival, Sally. It was such a magical evening. There was definitely something special in the air that night," he said.

"I know. But that's part of the beauty of our Festival. Everyone shares. There were several families who got toys for their children and clothes. One lady told me that her children would have a Christmas, thanks to us. That was a nice feeling."

"Yeah, it must've been. But you know others will have a nice Christmas just because they shopped at your store."

"Yes, of course, but they paid for it," she said with a chuckle.

"Yeah, they did, but you run a good store, Sally. I'm impressed with your prices and your friendliness. And believe me, I know."

"I know you do, Hunter. Your training and knowledge has been obvious from the start. I really appreciate it."

"Sweetheart, the pleasure's been all mine," he said with a warm smile.

Sally chuckled. "Oh, yes, I'm sure. Slaving for eleven hours day after day, waiting on people who don't even care how many hours you've worked. That wouldn't be high on many people's list of dream jobs."

"Want another piece?" he asked, indicating the pizza.

"Yes, thank you," she said, taking one.

He took a third piece and bit into it. "Mmm, this is good pizza. It's the best I've eaten in a while. Tell me, Sally, will you be serving something like this on Christmas Day?"

"No! I'm serving a traditional Christmas dinner with turkey and dressing."

"Ah, you're a Benjamin Franklin fan, are you?"

"What?"

"You know, Old Ben tried to convince everyone the turkey should be our National bird. Isn't that why we eat it on Thanksgiving and Christmas?"

"I guess so, but I'm serving turkey because that's what Mom used to serve."

"That's an even better reason, Sally, and I'm sure it will be good."

"What does your grandfather serve on Christmas?"

"He prefers steaks on Christmas Day."

"Steaks? I guess they are easier to clean up after. The turkey carcass is a pain sometimes."

"That's true, and you don't have a lot of leftovers with steaks."

"Yes, but I like the leftovers. It makes getting up the next morning fun. I love to have pie for breakfast on the day after Christmas."

Hunter leaned toward her. "Do you know that you are the sweetest person I've ever known?"

Sally sat back in surprise. "Why would you say that?"

"Because it's true. Now, do you want another piece of pizza?"

CHAPTER ELEVEN

WHEN they had finished Hunter waved to the waitress and asked her for a box to take the pizza with them. They soon had it packed up and were on their way again.

When they reached her house, Hunter parked the car and looked at her. "If I promise to behave, do I get to come in and help you bake cookies?"

"Of course you can, Hunter. I'd enjoy the company."

In the kitchen, Sally got out the things she'd need to bake sugar cookies. She mixed up a double batch of dough and then began to roll it out. Once she'd done that, she opened a drawer and took out cookie cutters in Christmas shapes. "Take your choice, Hunter."

He picked out four shapes he liked—a bell, a Christmas tree, Santa's head and a wreath.

"Those are my favorites, too. We'll just use those four."

They began cutting out cookies and placing them on the nearby cookie sheet. They filled two sheets and put them in the oven. Then Sally mixed colored icing to spread on the cookies.

They spent the rest of the evening decorating cookies

in bright colors. Hunter discovered he had quite a talent for decorating cookies. Sally encouraged him to experiment. One or two turned out badly, but he ate those.

When ten o'clock rolled around, Sally put the cookies away to save for Christmas Day.

"Thanks for all your help, Hunter. This was fun."

"Yes, it was. Will you put some cookies in my lunch tomorrow?"

"Just a couple. I don't want to spoil you, you know!"

He put his arms around her. "I should've known you'd be one of those mothers who refuses to spoil her child." He bent down and kissed her.

"You're not my child, Hunter!" Sally responded breathlessly.

"Always point out the technical details!" And he kissed her again.

"Hunter, I think you'd better go home. It's getting late."

"Okay, give me a goodbye kiss and I'll be on my way."

"But I've already given you two kisses."

"Yes, but those were just playful kisses. I want a real goodbye kiss."

She slid her arms around his neck and opened her mouth to his for a deep, satisfying kiss. So satisfying that she didn't want it to end.

When he pulled her arms down and backed away, she watched him wistfully.

"Don't look at me that way, Sally, or I'll throw you over my shoulder and go upstairs with you. I've got to go while I can. Good night, sweetheart."

Then he was out the door and in his car.

Sally leaned against the door, listening to him leave, a smile on her lips.

Sally had been right about the traffic they had in the store the next day. It was much less than the previous week. They only had a few gift-wraps they had to do. People were rushing in for something they'd forgotten or for the details everyone forgot until they needed them, like parcel tape and ribbons.

Susie was bored and Sally gave her a new project of re-arranging the children's department. They normally didn't carry a lot of toys and had sold out most of what they had. Sally asked her to do an arrangement of clothing to take up some of the empty space.

With Hunter, Mary and Ethel on the floor, Sally re-treated to the break room and worked on the books. She'd fallen behind on that kind of work during the rush. Hunter had been right—they had done well this Christmas season. She readied a bank deposit and put it in her purse. She tried never to carry a bank bag when she went to the bank. That made it much too obvious what she was doing, and as safe as Bailey was, she wasn't about to take any chances.

In fact, for some reason today she stopped by Hunter's side as he finished with a customer. "Hunter, would you like to go for a walk?"

He frowned but said, "Sure, that would be good. Where are we going?"

She leaned in and whispered, "Actually I'm going to the

bank, but don't feel like going alone today," and waited for his reaction.

"Yes, I'd definitely like to go for a walk."

She told Ethel she and Hunter were going to take a short walk to arouse their appetites and they walked out of the store.

"Is this how you handle trips to the bank?" Hunter whispered.

"No, not usually. I never do it at regular times. But what I'm taking today is exceptionally large. We've done well the past few days."

The bank was only a few storefronts down from the general store and they reached it quickly. There were a few customers in the bank, but Sally and Hunter didn't have to wait long to get served. Sally had filled out a deposit slip in the store and had everything ready to go. She stepped up to a window and drew out the pile of cash from her purse.

The teller, an old friend, had just counted out the money to verify the amount of the deposit and given Sally a receipt, when a man entered the bank with a scarf over the lower half of his face and yelled, "Okay, everybody stay calm and nobody gets hurt!" He was brandishing a pistol of some kind in his hand and everyone froze.

Hunter had been leaning nonchalantly against a pillar near the front door and Sally turned around to see where he was, praying that he wouldn't do anything to stop the bank robber.

But Hunter wasn't sharing her thoughts. He immediately grabbed for the gun the man was holding, taking both the gun and the man down to the floor. He was joined in his attempt to disarm the man by the bank president.

Sally stood paralyzed by Hunter's action until she heard a gunshot. The robber, in the struggle, had managed to fire the gun and Sally flew to the pile of men on the floor, desperate to see Hunter.

"You got him?" Hunter asked the bank president and several others who had come to their aid. He was holding his arm and blood was beginning to appear between his fingers.

"Hunter!" Sally cried out. "You're injured!"

"Yeah, but I don't think it's serious," Hunter assured her, which did nothing at all to relieve her anxieties.

"We've got to get you to the hospital," she said, putting her arm around him.

"Sure, we'll go in a little while," he said, sounding unconcerned.

By that time, the sheriff and a deputy had arrived and took the man into custody. The bank president, Gerald Hornwright, insisted on walking Hunter to the clinic the only doctor in Bailey ran. So the two of them, each holding on to Hunter, walked him down the street, drawing a slight crowd.

When they reached the clinic, Gerald held the door open and they entered, with Hunter dripping blood on their clean floor.

"Whoa! What happened?" the nurse asked as she reached for a cloth and immediately wrapped Hunter's hand in it. "Sit down here," she said, indicating a nearby chair. Gerald explained what had happened.

By that time, the doctor had come from his office and

began cleaning Hunter's wound. Fortunately the bullet had gone straight through Hunter's arm, leaving a clean wound that the doctor could easily fix. After cleaning it up and giving Hunter a tetanus shot, the doctor bandaged Hunter's arm.

"Okay, you're good to go, Mr Bedford. You'll need to get that checked in a week, after changing the bandage and making sure it's clean. You can handle that, can't you?"

"Sure, Doc."

"Here are the pain pills I'm prescribing and an antibiotic for infection, too. You'll need to take them as prescribed and get plenty of rest."

"I'll take care of him," Sally promised. "Hunter, do you want me to go get my car, so you won't have to walk?"

"Come on, Sally, it's not that far back to the store."

She didn't intend for him to go back to the store. She'd already decided that Hunter would be staying at her house until he had fully recovered from his ordeal. When she led him from the clinic, people were standing out on the sidewalk, having heard about the robbery. They clapped as Hunter and Sally appeared.

"This is embarrassing," he muttered.

"They just want to say thank you. A lot of their money is in the bank. You did them a favor."

"Aw, Sally, I just did what anyone would do. He wasn't a very big man."

"I know, Hunter, but sometimes, desperation makes people impossible to control. That was a dangerous thing you did if not a little stupid."

"He wasn't that strong. I think he was very nervous. Poor guy."

"How can you say that when you got shot? Do you want me to call your grandfather?"

"Uh, no, Sally, I don't."

"But, surely he'd like to know that you got hurt?"

"Probably better that he doesn't know it at all. Hey, where are we going?" Hunter asked as Sally steered him to the street behind the store.

"I'm taking you to my house. You can't work at the store the rest of the day. You need to lie down and get some rest. After all, you lost some blood."

"Come on, Sally, I lost maybe a thimbleful of blood. I don't need to lie down."

"I think the doctor said for you to rest."

"Then I should go to my room at the bed-and-breakfast."

"No, you'll need to have your bandage changed and you can't do that yourself, someone would have to do it for you. That will be my job. But first, I'm going to put you in bed and let you take a nap."

"Sally, I'm not a baby."

"I know, Hunter. Come on. We're almost there."

When they reached her house, she unlocked the front door and took him up the stairs to the bedrooms, leading him into the first room. Sally quickly turned down the bedding and Hunter had to silently admit the bed looked very comfortable and he was suddenly feeling a little weary.

"Strip down and get under the covers. I'm going to fix you something to drink and maybe a few cookies to eat. You need something to get your blood sugar back up to normal," Sally said, turning toward Hunter.

"Cookies sound good," Hunter muttered before he did as Sally asked.

When she returned a few minutes later, she propped him up and sat beside him as he sipped a cup of coffee and ate some cookies. Then he took the pain pill and the antibiotic the doctor had given him.

"This tastes good, Sally," Hunter said.

"I'm glad. I'll be back to check on you later." Then, much to Hunter's surprise, she bent and kissed him on his forehead. "Now, get some sleep."

She took the cup and saucer and went downstairs after pulling the door behind her.

Hunter lay there, feeling a little drowsy in spite of his protests. His wound hadn't seemed that big a deal when he'd felt the bullet sear his skin, but now it ached. He let his eyelids drift down and that was all he remembered.

Fortunately the store wasn't too busy that afternoon, though it was a little heavier than Sally had expected because everyone wanted to hear about the attempted bank robbery. They all asked about Hunter and Sally patiently told them all it wasn't serious, but she'd taken him into her house until he recovered, explaining that he would need to have his bandage changed.

"Sally, I know you have good intentions, but you be careful having a man in your house. People might talk, you know," one lady said, looking at Sally seriously.

"You know, Edith, I'm going to take care of Hunter because I owe him. If people want to gossip about that, then let them," Sally said, suddenly not caring about what people might think.

"Well, for that matter, we all owe Hunter. I mean, the insurance would've covered any funds lost, but it would take a few days, especially with Christmas coming. We've been through that before."

"I know. He should've remained still and let the man steal the money, but that's not Hunter. So I'm taking care of him."

The old lady smiled and nodded at Sally, as if she sensed there was something more going on here than just looking after a local hero. That evening when they closed the store at seven, Sally didn't linger. She hurried home to check on Hunter and to cook a good dinner for him. Hoping he'd feel like eating, she took two steaks and put them on to grill before she went up the stairs to check on him.

When she opened the door, he was sound asleep. She checked to be sure he wasn't running a fever, but he seemed to be all right. Gently shaking him, she called his name. Hunter slowly opened his eyes and looked around the room. "Hey, Sally. What happened? Where am I?"

"You were wounded in the robbery attempt and the doctor said you should rest. I gave you the pills he gave me and you've been sleeping all afternoon. Are you feeling better?"

"Yeah, I guess so. Where are my pants?"

"Over here. I've started dinner and you need to eat something to keep your strength up. Why don't you get dressed and come down as soon as you feel like it. You're due another pain pill. I'll give it to you when you get downstairs."

"Okay."

Sally left him and went down the stairs to finish making dinner. She'd just reached the kitchen when there was a knock on her door. Turning back, she opened the door to discover the mayor of Bailey standing there.

"Hi, Sally. I'm sorry to disturb you, but I understand Hunter is staying here with you?"

"Yes, I moved him in this afternoon so I can keep an eye on him until he's well enough to go back to Denver."

"That's good and very generous of you. May I speak to him, please?"

"Just a minute and I'll go get him. Won't you come in?"

"Yes, thank you, Sally."

Sally walked to the bottom of the stairs. "Hunter? The mayor is here to see you. Are you coming down?"

"Yes, I'm coming," she heard him say faintly.

When he finally appeared, Hunter had donned his slacks and dress shirt.

"Hunter, I'm Richard Grant, the mayor of Bailey. I just wanted to thank you for risking your life to stop the robbery. We appreciate your courage."

"He was kind of little, Mr Grant. I didn't risk that much."

"Well, I'm not sure other people would have been as quick to jump in so on behalf of the town, I just wanted to express our appreciation."

"Thank you. That's very thoughtful of you."

The two men shook hands and then Richard said goodbye to Sally and left.

Sally went to the kitchen without saying anything. Hunter followed.

"What was that all about?" Hunter asked.

"What do you mean?"

"The mayor coming here. Why did he do that?"

"I thought he told you he wanted to express appreciation for your courage." She was washing some broccoli before putting it on to steam.

"Yeah, but—it wasn't that big a deal."

Sally smiled without turning around. "Whatever you say, Hunter. I've got your pain pills over here. Are you ready for one?"

"Maybe I'd better save it until I get ready for bed. I might need it more then."

Sally put the broccoli in the steamer and added water. Hunter sat down at the kitchen table and poured himself a glass of water. "It was nice of you to bring me here today, Sally. But you should have sent me to the bed-and-breakfast. I would've managed."

"You're not going back to the bed-and-breakfast. I packed your bags and loaded your car and drove it over here. You'll stay here until you go home to Denver."

He stared at her, stunned by her announcement.

She looked at him. "What?"

"What are you doing, Sally? Aren't you worried that everyone will say we're—you know, sleeping together."

"But they'd be wrong, wouldn't they, Hunter? It's all right. I know you don't have any serious interest in me."

"Oh? How do you know?" Hunter said, suddenly looking at Sally closely.

"Come on, Hunter. You're big city and I'm small town. We come form different worlds. You have to leave for Denver in a few days whether you really want to or not—you'll have to go back. It's your home. But, while you're here I'll take care of you to repay you for all the work you've done for me. It's only fair," Sally said, smiling at Hunter.

CHAPTER TWELVE

SALLY was up at her normal time the next day, but she didn't expect Hunter to be up as early. She had given him his pills before he had gone to bed last night and she suspected he would sleep until she awakened him.

Sally made a lunch for Hunter and covered it with plastic wrap and put it in the refrigerator. Then she fixed a tray for Hunter's breakfast.

Sally ate her own breakfast and then she readied a fresh bandage and Hunter's two pills that he needed to take this morning. Sally carried it up the stairs and knocked on his door before she opened it and went in.

"Hunter? Are you awake?"

She knew he wasn't, but he quickly stirred and sat up in bed, looking around. Sally set the tray down on the desk and picked up the bandage, the hydrogen peroxide for cleaning the wound and the pills, along with the glass of juice.

"What time is it?" he asked groggily.

"It's almost nine o'clock. If you can sit up a little, I'll clean your wound and redo the bandage," she said, handing him the glass of juice.

"But I need to get dressed. The store opens in a few minutes."

"You're not going to work today, Hunter. Your arm needs to heal and that won't happen if you're up moving around."

"It's not that bad a wound, Sally. I can work—"

"No, you can't." She propped several pillows behind him and unwrapped the bandage on his arm. Then she put some hydrogen peroxide on some cotton and cleaned the wound. After that, she wrapped the wound in a clean bandage.

"Now, you need to take these two pills."

"I don't need the pain pill, Sally. It makes me groggy!"

"But you're not getting out of bed today anyway, so it will be all right if it makes you sleepy."

"I have to go to the bathroom," Hunter then said, stubbornly.

"Okay. I'll go down and get the mystery book you were reading while you go to the bathroom. Then I'll come back and give you your pills and your breakfast."

"Sally, you don't need to wait on me. I can manage."

"Go," she ordered and got up and left the room.

Hunter didn't wait. He didn't want to get caught in his underwear. He wanted to take a shower, but he wasn't sure what to do about his wound.

When he heard Sally's steps on the stairs, he rushed back to his bed and slid into place under the cover as she came into the room.

"Here's the mystery when you wake up and want to have something to do. Now, take the pills."

He did as she ordered, sipping the orange juice she offered from the breakfast tray. Then he ate his scrambled eggs, bacon and toast. There was also a cup of coffee. He eagerly reached for it and discovered it was decaf. "I don't get real coffee?"

"I want you to sleep, not stay awake."

He put the coffee cup back on the tray.

"All right. When you wake up for lunch, you'll find it wrapped up in the fridge if I haven't made it back yet."

"Okay."

She leaned over and kissed his forehead again. It seemed to be a habit now. Hunter was tempted to catch her shoulders and bring her mouth to his, but he didn't think that would be a such a good idea, especially as he was in bed.

"I'll come check on you around noon."

"Okay," he said, picking up the mystery novel.

After she left the house, Hunter put the book down. It was too hard to hold it up to read. Besides, he was a little sleepy.

Sally was a little late opening the store, but except for Billy waiting on her, there wasn't anyone else wanting to come in. She tidied the store, missing Hunter's cheerful presence and help. With a sigh, she reminded herself that she should get used to being alone again.

When the bell over the door rang, she looked up to see a customer come in. "Let me know if I can help you," she called, smiling.

She didn't recognize the man, but occasionally they had strangers wander in. He was looking over the entire store. It reminded Sally of Hunter's arrival, when he had wanted to talk to her about the agreement his grandfather and her father had had. She thought back to that first meeting and how much had happened in that short time.

The man came closer. "Are you Sally Rogers?"

"Yes, I am. How can I help you?"

"What have you done to my grandson?"

Sally went completely still. Then she looked at the man. "Your grandson is in bed at the moment in my house, Mr Hunt. Would you like to see him?"

"Of course I would! I called the bed-and-breakfast at seven this morning and was told he'd moved out—into your house!"

"That's right, and did they tell you why?"

"No! And I didn't ask! I'm not an idiot, Miss Rogers, I know why a man moves into a young woman's house!"

In spite of his anger, Sally calmly said, "I moved him to my house so I could change his bandage and keep his wound clean."

"What wound?" The old man actually looked frightened then.

"Hunter tried to stop a bank robbery yesterday, Mr Hunt, and was wounded. It's not serious as long as the wound is kept clean and he doesn't get an infection. Right now, he's taking pain pills, which keep him sleeping. If you can wait twenty minutes, someone will be here to relieve me and I can take you over to see him."

"Fine! I'll wait, but I don't like it!"

"I perfectly understand," Sally said and returned to folding the jeans, watching Mr Hunt out of the corner of her eye. He wandered the store, picking up objects and studying them, then replacing them on the shelf.

"Do you sell many of these?" he asked, holding up some books she'd ordered just before the Christmas rush. There were only two on the shelf.

"Yes, I ordered fifteen before Christmas. That's all that's left."

"Hmm," was all the old man said before he continued his perusal of the store.

A few minutes later, the bell on the front door rang and Ethel, Mary and Susie all came in.

Sally went to meet them and explained what she was going to do. Then she turned to Wilbur Hunt. "Mr Hunt, if you'll come with me, I'll take you to see Hunter."

The man turned to follow Sally, never saying anything and she led him across the street to her home and unlocked the door. Then she went up the stairs, calling as she did so, "Hunter? Are you awake?"

When she reached the bedroom, she realized Hunter was soundly asleep.

Sally stepped aside and allowed his grandfather to see his grandson.

"Hunter? Wake up, boy!"

Sally watched as Hunter frowned, but he didn't open his eyes.

Mr Hunt grabbed Hunter's arm. Unfortunately it was his injured arm. Sally stepped forward urgently to stop him and pulled the man's hand back quickly. "Not that arm, sir! It's his injured one."

"What? Oh, sorry, but I need the boy to wake up."

Hunter answered him. "I'm awake, Granddad, but what are you doing here?"

"Trying to keep you from making a big mistake!"

"What are you talking about?" Hunter demanded.

"I need you to get up and get dressed. I'm taking you home this very instant."

"Mr Hunt, that's not necessary!" Sally protested.

"She's right. It isn't necessary." Hunter gave his grandfather a level look. "I'm fine here. Sally is taking care of me, and I'll be back on my feet by tomorrow."

"Don't be silly. I'm not letting you throw your life away on a store like hers. Or on a woman like her. You need to come home, now!"

Hunter looked at Sally. "Sally, honey, would you mind if I talked to my grandfather alone for a minute?"

"No, I don't mind. I'll go down to the kitchen."

Once Sally went downstairs, Hunter pushed another pillow behind him and sat up enough to face his grandfather. "Granddad, I'm not coming home with you. I've found where I want to be and it's here, in Sally's store. I can do all the things I like, and less of what I don't like. And I've fallen in love with Sally."

"This is nonsense! She's just after your money! Why else would a small-town girl bring a man into her house?"

"I didn't say she's in love with me. I hope she is, but I don't really know. But she's not after my money. She's doing pretty well on her own here, actually. Her store is very productive."

"Productive? It's half empty!"

"Yeah, the rush is over now. She did a great job of ordering to meet the needs of her shoppers in plenty of time. She had to reorder last week. I'd say that's good planning wouldn't you?"

Hunter's grandfather turned to look out of the window that overlooked Sally's store. "I still say you're crazy."

"Granddad, I love you, but I'm not the corporate guy you want. I'd be miserable working in the offices and either go crazy within five years, or I'd walk out. Here, I'm happy. I've never been so happy," Hunter said softly.

Mr Hunt turned to face his grandson. "Okay, if that's how you feel, come home and clear your head first. Think about this before you do anything rash. Anyway, you are hurt, you can't help her in this state. Why don't you come home to recover? No use burdening the girl like you are now."

"No. My head is clear and I know Sally doesn't feel burdened. I'll come home for Christmas dinner and I'll bring Sally with me, if that's okay. I'll even come back to town for board meetings once a month. But that's enough. I'm going to be a resident of Bailey from now on."

"We'll see!" Mr Hunt spun around and went down the stairs. At the bottom, he called out, "Miss Rogers?"

Sally came out of the kitchen. "Yes, Mr Hunt?'

"Mind if I have a cup of coffee?"

"Of course not. Come into the kitchen."

Sally held open the door for him and then moved into the kitchen to pour him a cup of coffee. She added some cookies on a saucer for him.

"Miss Rogers, I need to take the boy home. I'll make sure he gets good care, but—well, to be honest, he tends to think he's fallen in love with any woman who cooks for him. Sorry about that, but that's the way he is," Mr Hunt said, staring into his coffee cup.

"I see," Sally answered.

"So I need to get him home and take care of him."

"I'm perfectly willing to take care of him here, Mr Hunt. He should be up and around by tomorrow. I owe him at least that much care. Besides, he's a hero to the townspeople."

"I'm taking him home!" the old man growled, staring at Sally.

"Okay, then I'll be glad to help you get him to the car…if that's what Hunter wants," Sally said, meeting the old man's angry gaze proudly. "I'll just run upstairs and talk to Hunter."

Sally didn't wait for the old man to answer. She was desperately hoping Hunter didn't want to go, but she couldn't think of any reason he wouldn't. When she got to his room, he was leaning against a pillow, his eyes closed.

"Your grandfather says you have to go home with him. Is that what you want, Hunter?" Sally asked nervously from the doorway.

"Not unless you're throwing me out," Hunter said, looking straight at Sally.

"He also said that you tend to fall in love with anyone who cooks for you. Have you fallen in love with the lady who runs the bed-and-breakfast?"

Hunter smiled at Sally before he spoke. "Nope. I haven't fallen for anyone at the Diamond Back, or the pizzaria, either. But I've fallen in love with you."

Sally blinked several times and swallowed. "Because I've cooked for you?"

"Nope. Because I think you're the most wonderful

woman in the world. I want to live with you for the rest of my life, here in Bailey and raise our four kids." He paused, his gaze devouring her. "What do you think, Sally? Will you marry me?"

"Oh, Hunter, I desperately want to, but you must be sure this is what you really want. I'd be devastated if you left me to go back to the city after a few months."

"Never, Sally, my love, I promise. Come closer. I've been afraid to kiss you, in case we got carried away, but I think this calls for getting a little carried away."

"I don't want you to hurt your arm," she cautioned, in spite of falling into his outstretched arms.

"You won't hurt my arm. You could never hurt me."

"Oh, Hunter! I've been falling in love with you, thinking you were leaving me for the big city. I was so unhappy!"

"Let's see if I can cheer you up," he whispered as he kissed her.

Several minutes later, Wilbur Hunt complained that they were ignoring him.

"We're trying, Granddad," Hunter said, looking over Sally's shoulder at his grandfather standing in the doorway.

"I told her I was taking you home."

"But you were wrong. I am home," he assured his grandfather, looking fondly at Sally.

"Hunter's going to help me run the store, Mr Hunt. We are going to do it together. I'm so happy!" Sally said, flinging her arms around Hunter's neck.

"He said he's bringing you to dinner Christmas night."

"Is that all right?" Sally asked.

Mr Hunt looked at the two young people on the bed

and shook his head. "Yes, you're both welcome. But this had better be a long engagement. I don't want you to make a mistake."

"I'm thinking about a short engagement, Granddad. I don't want her to get away." Hunter smiled at Sally. "And you know, Granddad, as soon as we can manage it, we'll probably be having babies. At least four. And no, the baby can't come live with you. He, or she, will be raised by his parents in small town Bailey. But maybe, if you're good, they'll come visit every once in a while."

"Four, huh? Maybe this marriage isn't such a bad idea after all. Maybe I'll build a retirement home here in Bailey," Wilbur muttered.

"You could consider that on your drive back to Denver," Hunter suggested.

"I'm not sure you two should be left alone."

"That's the only way you'll get those grandkids, Granddad."

"Definitely," Sally said. "I'm a little shy."

"Okay, okay. I get the hint. But you'll both come to dinner on Christmas Day?"

"We will. We should be there about six o'clock."

"Will you spend the night?"

"I can't. The store will be open the next morning," Sally said.

"Sorry, Granddad. Duty calls."

"All right, I'm going. I'll see both of you in a couple of days," the old man said and for the first time that day he smiled.

They didn't move, listening to his steps down the stairs.

When the door closed, Hunter whispered, "Do you think he's really gone?"

She tiptoed over to the window that looked out on the front of the street. "Yes, he's gone." She turned back to face Hunter. "Were you just pretending to propose so you could upset him?"

"No, sweetheart, I'd propose to you no matter who was here. I love you. I promise I'll be a good husband. I only want to live here with you, in Bailey, the rest of my life."

"Oh, Hunter," she said as she collapsed on the bed, her lips returning to his. Several minutes later, he pushed her away.

"Honey, I'd like to keep on kissing you, but my defenses are kind of weak because of those pills you gave me. I don't want to make love to you until we're safely married."

"Me, neither. But I do like kissing you," she said. "We could just try it one more time."

"Okay, one more time."

Sally returned to the store after giving Hunter his lunch. She joined him, eating upstairs, then she cleaned and changed his bandage and gave him two more pills.

When she entered the store later that day, she was smiling. Her staff wanted to know why she was so happy. She told them it was because the Christmas rush was almost over.

When the phone rang, she answered it, a trill in her voice.

"Sally? Is that you?"

"Hi, Penny! How are you?"

"Fine. Um, I wanted to ask you something."

"Of course, what?"

"May I bring Jake to Christmas dinner?"

"Certainly, if you want to."

"Yes, I do. We have something to tell you."

"Now?"

"No, I think it can wait until tomorrow."

"All right. Hunter will be joining us, too."

"He hasn't gone home yet?"

"No, not yet. He's decided to stay for a little longer. Will you both be here at noon?"

"Yes, we will. And I'll bring a cake for us all to eat after dinner."

"Okay, I'm looking forward to seeing you, Penny."

"Me, too, Sally."

Hunter came down to the kitchen while Sally prepared dinner that evening.

"Oh, Hunter, you were right."

"About what, sweetheart?"

"Penny called today."

"Jake is coming to Christmas dinner?" Hunter replied smiling.

"Yes, and they have news for us."

"What do you think?"

"I think they're engaged."

"Well, we'll have a surprise for them, too, won't we?"

"I know. We're going to need a bottle of champagne. Maybe you can go to the grocery store and buy a couple of bottles tomorrow."

"A *couple* of bottles? I can't drink that much and still drive to Denver."

"Oh, I forgot about that. Okay, just one bottle. And a bottle of cider. I like that better anyway."

"You're a cheap date," he said with a laugh. "Now I have something I want to talk to you about, something that my grandfather said. Will you let me buy into the store, Sally, so we can be equal partners?"

"That's not necessary, Hunter. If we marry, it automatically becomes half yours."

"I know. But I don't want you to think I married you to get part ownership of the store. Let me buy half of it. Then you won't ever have to worry. You can put the money in savings under your name. If you don't ever use it, we can divide it up among our children. It can provide for their college funds."

Sally looked at Hunter for a moment. This was going to be their first major decision that they would make together, and she was nervous and excited in equal measure. "I'm not sure that's something we need to do, Hunter. Who's going to be the boss if we each own fifty percent of the store?"

"Hmm, you've got a point. So you want me to just buy forty-nine percent?" Hunter said and Sally felt a tingle of electricity run down her spine. She didn't need to be nervous with Hunter, because he would clearly do anything to make her happy.

She bent down to kiss him. He pulled her into his lap. When he lifted his lips, he asked, "Is that what you want?"

"No, silly. I want you to buy fifty percent. If we don't agree, we'll negotiate. That's what Mom and Dad always did."

"I suspect you'll be able to persuade me very quickly."

"Oh, good!" she said, kissing him again before she returned to her cooking.

Christmas Day arrived and Sally and Hunter were in the kitchen together as Sally put the final touches on their Christmas dinner.

The dining room table was set with four places and a beautiful flower arrangement was in the center of the table. Already several dishes were on the sideboard. The turkey was waiting for Jake to carry it into the dining room. Sally had refused to let Hunter lift the turkey, afraid he'd hurt his arm again.

When the doorbell rang, she sent Hunter to answer it.

He swung open the door and found Penny and Jake on the doorstep. "Come on in. We've been anxiously awaiting you. Sally's in the kitchen."

"Are you Hunter?" Penny asked, staring at him.

He blinked. "Yes, I met you, remember?"

"Yes, but you were in the Santa Claus costume. We didn't have any idea what you looked like."

Hunter laughed, remembering the last time he had met Jake and Penny. "Sorry. I forgot about that."

They followed him into the kitchen. Sally greeted Penny with a hug. "Welcome, Jake. I'm glad you could come."

"I'm delighted to be here."

"Would you carry the turkey into the dining room? Since Hunter injured his arm, I didn't want him to try."

Jake looked at Hunter, a frown on his face. "You hurt yourself?"

"Didn't you hear?" Sally asked. "Hunter brought down a bank robber, but he got shot in the arm. He's the town hero."

"Come on, Sally. I told you he was a little guy." Hunter actually looked embarrassed.

Sally laughed. "You still got hurt."

"Yeah, I did, just a little," he admitted. "But I had a good nurse," he continued, smiling teasingly at Sally.

Jake carried the turkey through to the dining room and they all gathered around the table. Sally stuck out her hands to the person on each side of her. "I think it's important that we stay connected, especially this year. So I'd like us to hold hands while we ask the blessing for today."

After they'd said the blessing and filled their plates, they all sat down at the table. That's when Sally saw the diamond band Penny was wearing. "Penny! Where did you get that beautiful band?"

Penny looked at her finger, bending it several times. "Dad bought it for Mom to replace her gold band for Christmas. I found it when I was clearing through their things. But, well, actually, I'm going to use it for my wedding band—Jake and I are engaged."

"Oh, Penny! Congratulations!" Sally said, jumping up to hug Penny. "That's such good news and a wonderful surprise. I am so pleased for you both," Sally said, wiping tears of joy from her eyes. When she sat back down at the table, she looked at Hunter, who was smiling at her fondly. "Actually, there is something I have to tell you, too. Hunter and I are engaged as well."

"No!" Penny shouted and ran to hug Sally.

"Wait a minute," Jake said. "Why are we being left out of the hugging?"

"You've got me." Hunter stood and hugged Jake. "But you know, it might be more fun if we hugged them."

"Good thinking." Jake hugged Penny and Hunter hugged Sally.

When they all sat back down, Hunter stood again. He walked around the table to Sally. "You won't believe this, but the day I went back home, after meeting you, I got this for you." He set a small box down beside her.

She looked at him, her eyes wide. "What is it?"

"Open it and see."

Sally, her hands shaking, picked up the box and opened it. She stared at the contents, her hands starting to shake badly.

"A—a ring! A beautiful ring." She looked at Hunter.

"Try it on. We may have to have it sized."

She slid the ring on her third finger, left hand. "It—it fits!"

"That was my grandmother's ring. She left it for me. I should've known it would be a perfect fit."

"Oh, Hunter!" Sally flung her arms around his neck and he held her in his arms.

When, after several kisses, they settled down at the table again, Hunter asked Jake the all-important question. "When are you two planning on getting married?"

"New Year's Day. We want to start the year together."

"Hey, that's a great idea. Sally? How do you feel about that?"

"I think that's a wonderful idea. Could we organize something in time?"

"I don't see why not. In fact, we could get married on

New Year's Eve and drive to Denver for a four-day weekend. My condo has two bedrooms. We could share our honeymoon, too."

"I like that idea. What do you think, Jake?" Penny aksed.

"Sounds good to me," Jake agreed, smiling. "As long as you're happy with it."

"Good answer," Hunter agreed.

"It's the key for marital happiness. My dad told me a long time ago," Jake explained.

"Okay, let's get down to planning our special day," Penny said.

Six days later, Jake and Penny and Hunter and Sally gathered with their friends and families in front of the pastor of the Bailey Friendship Church. From a simple ceremony with each couple being the other's witnesses, they found themselves with volunteers standing up with them. Dusty stood beside Jake, and Chris stood by Hunter. Penny's housekeeper, Harriet, was Penny's bridesmaid, and Linda was Sally's.

Hunter's grandfather sat in the front row next to Jake's parents, and the rest of the church was filled with the citizens of Bailey.

When the final words were spoken, the pastor had the two couples face their audience.

"Ladies and gentlemen, I present Mr and Mrs Jake Larson and Mr and Mrs Hunter Bedford. May God bless their unions."

Applause erupted in the church. When they started down the aisle, the two ladies were on the inside and they clasped hands with each other joining the four of them as they stepped into the new year, no longer alone and with their own new family.

Their hearts were overflowing with love.

* * * * *

Kimberley Blackstone didn't notice the waiting horde of media until it was too late. Flashbulbs exploded around her like a New Year's light show. She skidded to a halt, so abruptly her trailing suitcase all but overtook her.

This had to be a case of mistaken identity. Surely. Kimberley hadn't been on the paparazzi hit list for close to a decade, not since she'd estranged herself from her billionaire father and his headline-hungry diamond business.

But no, it was *her* name they called. *Her* face was the focus of a swarm of lenses that circled her like avid hornets. Her heart started to pound with fear-fueled adrenaline.

What did they want?

What was going on?

With a rising sense of bewilderment she scanned the crowd for a clue, and her gaze fastened on a tall, leonine figure forcing his way to the front. A tall, familiar figure. Her head came up in stunned recognition, and their gazes collided across the sea of heads before the cameras erupted with another barrage of flashes, this time right in her exposed face.

Blinded by the flashbulbs—and by the shock of that momentary eye-meet—Kimberley didn't realize his intent until he'd forged his way to her side, possibly by the sheer strength of his personality. She felt his arm wrap around her shoulder, pulling her into the protective shelter of his body, allowing her no time to object. No chance to lift her hands to ward him off.

In the space of a hastily drawn breath, she found herself plastered knee-to-nose against six feet two inches of hard-bodied male.

Ric Perrini.

Her lover for ten torrid weeks, her husband for ten tumultuous days.

Her ex for ten tranquil years.

After all this time, he should not have felt so familiar but, oh dear, he did. She knew the scent of that body and its lean, muscular strength. She knew its heat and its slick power and every response it could draw from hers.

She also recognized the ease with which he'd taken control of the moment and the decisiveness of his deep voice when it rumbled close to her ear. "I have a car waiting outside. Is this your only luggage?"

Kimberley nodded. "I assume you will tell me," she said tightly, "what this welcome party is all about."

"Not while the welcome party is within earshot. No."

Barking a request for the cameramen to stand aside, Perrini took her hand and pulled her into step with his ground-eating stride. Kimberley let him, because he was right, damn his arrogant, Italian-suited hide. Despite the speed with which he whisked her across the airport terminal, she could almost feel the hot breath of the pursuing media on her back.

This was neither the time nor the place for explanations. Inside his car, however, she would get answers.

Now that the initial shock had been blown away—by the haste of their retreat, by the heat of her gathering indignation, by the rush of adrenaline fired by Perrini's presence and the looming verbal battle—her brain was starting to tick over. This had to be her father's doing. And if it was a Howard Blackstone publicity ploy, then it had to be about Blackstone Diamonds, the company that ruled his life.

The knowledge made her chest tighten with a familiar ache of disillusionment.

She'd known her father would be flying in from Sydney for today's opening of the newest in his chain of exclusive, high-end jewelry boutiques. The opulent shopfront sat adjacent to the rival business where Kimberley worked. No coincidence, she thought bitterly, just as it was no coincidence that Ric Perrini was here in Auckland ushering her to his car.

Perrini was Howard Blackstone's right-hand man, second in command at Blackstone Diamonds, a legacy of his short-lived marriage to the boss's daughter. No doubt her father had sent him to fetch her; the question was *why?*

* * * * *

Get swept away down under with the glitz and glamour of the Blackstone empire as Kimberley tries to determine the real reason behind her "reunion" with Ric....

*Look for VOWS & A VENGEFUL GROOM
by Bronwyn Jameson,
in stores January 2008.*

When Kimberley Blackstone's father is
presumed dead, Kimberley is required to take
over the helm of Blackstone Diamonds. She
has to work closely with her ex, Ric Perrini, to
battle not only the press, but also the fierce
attraction still sizzling between them. Does Ric
feel the same...or is it the power her share of
Blackstone Diamonds will provide him as he
battles for boardroom supremacy.

Look for

VOWS &
A VENGEFUL GROOM

by

BRONWYN
JAMESON

Available January wherever you buy books

To fulfill his father's dying wish,
Greek tycoon Christos Niarchos must
marry Ava Monroe, a woman who
betrayed him years ago. But his soon-to-
be-wife has a secret that could rock
more than his passion for her.

Look for

THE GREEK
TYCOON'S
SECRET HEIR

by

KATHERINE
GARBERA

Available January wherever you buy books

REQUEST YOUR FREE BOOKS!
2 FREE NOVELS PLUS 2
FREE GIFTS!

HARLEQUIN ROMANCE®

From the Heart, For the Heart

YES! Please send me 2 FREE Harlequin Romance® novels and my 2 FREE gifts. After receiving them, if I don't wish to receive any more books, I can return the shipping statement marked "cancel." If I don't cancel, I will receive 4 brand-new novels every month and be billed just $3.57 per book in the U.S., or $4.05 per book in Canada, plus 25¢ shipping and handling per book and applicable taxes, if any*. That's a savings of over 15% off the cover price! I understand that accepting the 2 free books and gifts places me under no obligation to buy anything. I can always return a shipment and cancel at any time. Even if I never buy another book from Harlequin, the two free books and gifts are mine to keep forever.   114 HDN EEV7 314 HDN EEWK

Name	(PLEASE PRINT)	
Address		Apt.
City	State/Prov.	Zip/Postal Code

Signature (if under 18, a parent or guardian must sign)

Mail to the **Harlequin Reader Service®:**
IN U.S.A.: P.O. Box 1867, Buffalo, NY 14240-1867
IN CANADA: P.O. Box 609, Fort Erie, Ontario L2A 5X3

Not valid to current Harlequin Romance subscribers.

Want to try two free books from another line?
Call 1-800-873-8635 or visit www.morefreebooks.com.

* Terms and prices subject to change without notice. NY residents add applicable sales tax. Canadian residents will be charged applicable provincial taxes and GST. This offer is limited to one order per household. All orders subject to approval. Credit or debit balances in a customer's account(s) may be offset by any other outstanding balance owed by or to the customer. Please allow 4 to 6 weeks for delivery.

Your Privacy: Harlequin is committed to protecting your privacy. Our Privacy Policy is available online at www.eHarlequin.com or upon request from the Reader Service. From time to time we make our lists of customers available to reputable firms who may have a product or service of interest to you. If you would prefer we not share your name and address, please check here. ☐

HR07

Inside ROMANCE

Stay up-to-date on all your romance reading news!

Inside Romance is a FREE quarterly newsletter highlighting our upcoming series releases and promotions.

Visit

www.eHarlequin.com/InsideRomance

to sign up to receive our complimentary newsletter today!

IRNJ1107

HARLEQUIN

//// NASCAR

Ladies, start your engines!
Pulse-accelerating dramas centered on four **NASCAR** families and the racing season that will test them all!

On the eve of a new NASCAR season, everything is falling apart for Kent Grosso: a blackmailer is threatening to ruin his reputation on the track, and Kent's girlfriend, Tanya Wells, is questioning his honesty. It's up to Kent to prove to everyone just what he is capable of—as a driver and as a man.

Feel the RUSH on and off the track.

Visit www.GetYourHeartRacing.com for all of the latest details.

NASCAR21784

Coming Next Month

Start your New Year with a bang with six terrific reads, only from Harlequin Romance®.

#3997 HER HAND IN MARRIAGE Jessica Steele

Get ready for the perfect English gentleman to sweep you off your feet! Romillie never imagined that a high-flying executive like Naylor would be interested in an ordinary girl like her, but she's bowled over when he whisks her away to his beautiful Cotswold cottage....

#3998 THE RANCHER'S DOORSTEP BABY Patricia Thayer
Western Weddings

Does the image of a man cradling a tiny baby in his arms melt your heart? You aren't alone! Rachel isn't sure whether drifter Cole will stick around for long, but seeing the tender way he holds her delicate baby, she knows her heart belongs to him forever.

#3999 THE SHEIKH'S UNSUITABLE BRIDE Liz Fielding
Desert Brides

Have you ever wanted someone you really shouldn't have? Desert prince Zahir knows Diana is not what his family and country expect in a wife. But this thoroughly unsuitable woman, whose eyes sparkle with mischief, is worth breaking the rules for.

#4000 THE BRIDESMAID'S BEST MAN Barbara Hannay

One special night between rugged best man Mark and beautiful bridesmaid Sophie seemed to be all they would get to share, as Mark had to return home to Australia. But now it seems these two will be sharing the most special job of all—parenthood!

#4001 MOONLIGHT AND ROSES Jackie Braun

Jaye thought she knew what she wanted from life—her career, and the freedom to be her own woman. But the intoxicating mix of new business partner Zack, the glimmer of moonlight and the scent of roses in the air is making her change her mind....

#4002 A MOTHER IN A MILLION Melissa James
Heart to Heart

How can you be sure that someone loves you—really loves *you*? Jennifer's heart goes out to single dad Noah and his motherless children, but when he proposes, Jennifer wants to be sure he wants her as his wife, not just as a mother to his children.

HRCNM1207